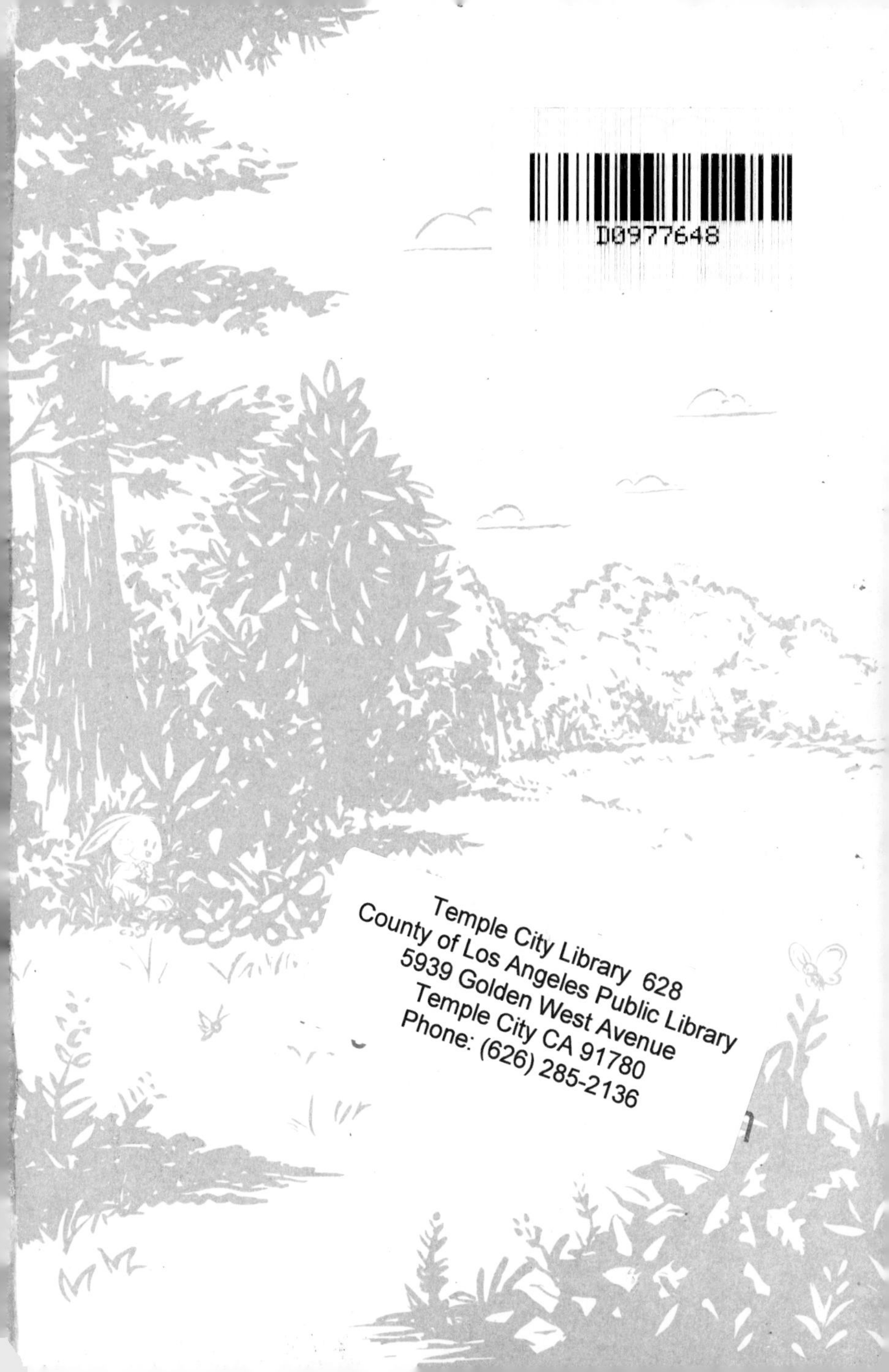

# OWLY ™

## JUST A LITTLE BLUE

# ANDY RUNTON

# OWLY:

## VOLUME TWO, JUST A LITTLE BLUE



ISBN 1-891830-64-3

1. ALL-AGES
2. ORNITHOLOGY
3. GRAPHIC NOVELS

TOP SHELF PRODUCTIONS
P.O. BOX 1282
MARIETTA, GA 30061-1282
U.S.A.

WWW.TOPSHELFCOMIX.COM

PUBLISHED IN 2005 BY TOP SHELF PRODUCTIONS, INC.
PUBLISHERS: CHRIS STAROS AND BRETT WARNOCK.


EDITED BY CHRIS STAROS & ROBERT VENDITTI

FIRST PRINTING, MARCH 2005
PRINTED IN CANADA

OTHER BOOKS BY ANDY RUNTON:

OWLY: THE WAY HOME & THE BITTERSWEET SUMMER
ISBN 1-891830-62-7

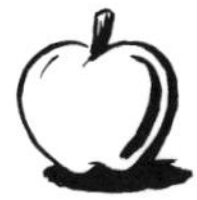

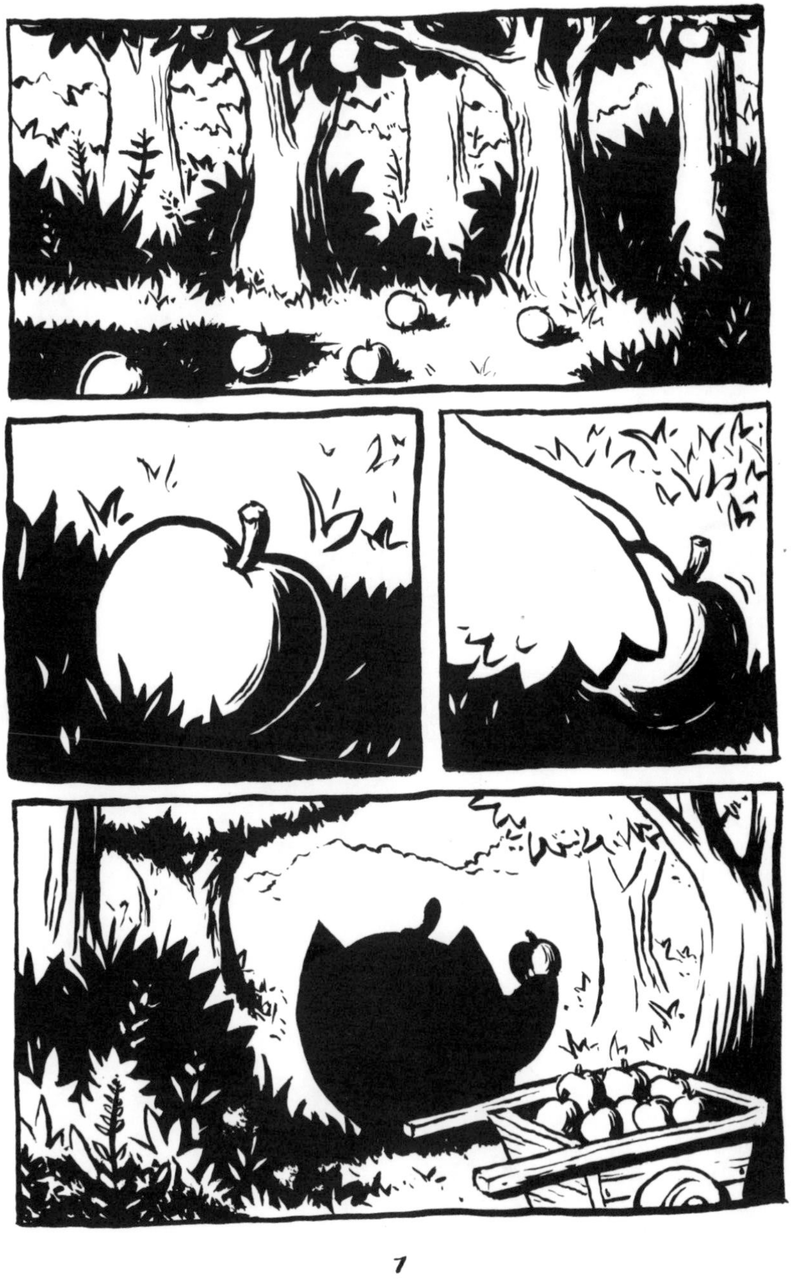

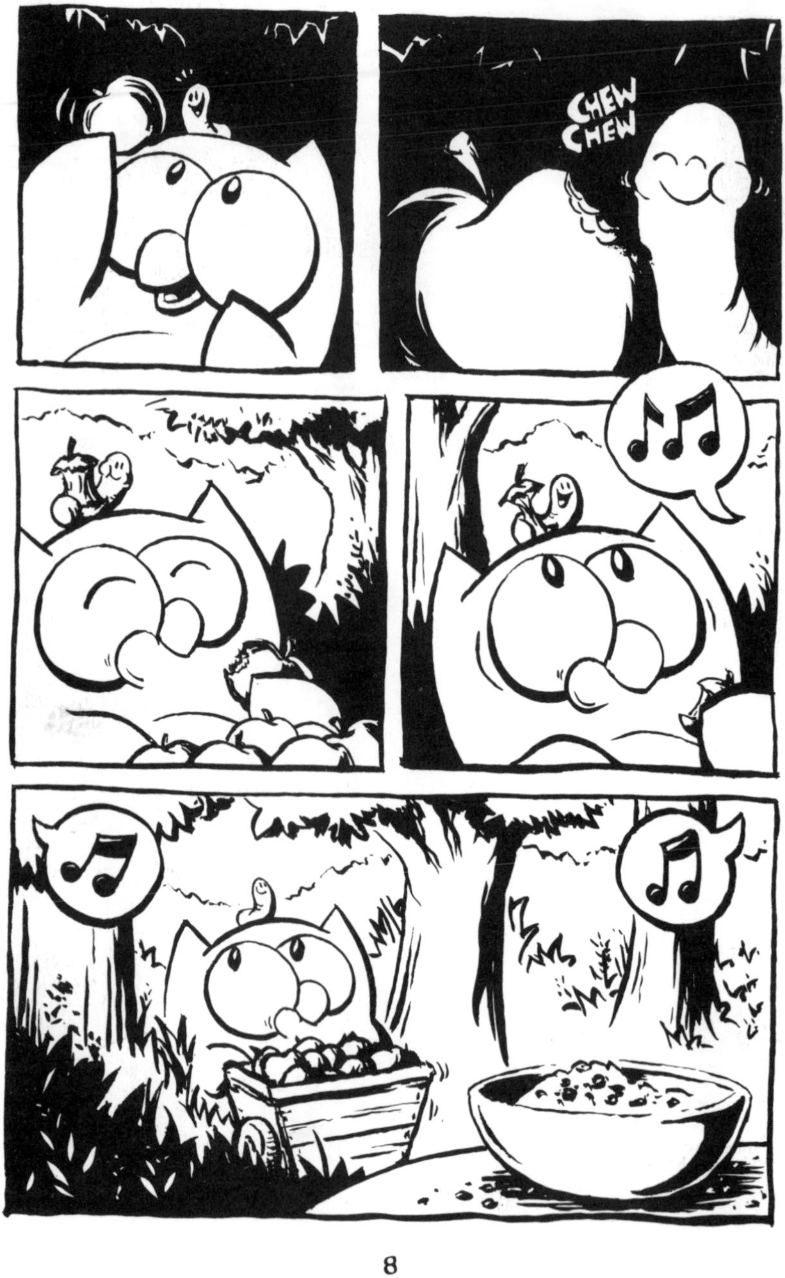
CHEW
CHEW

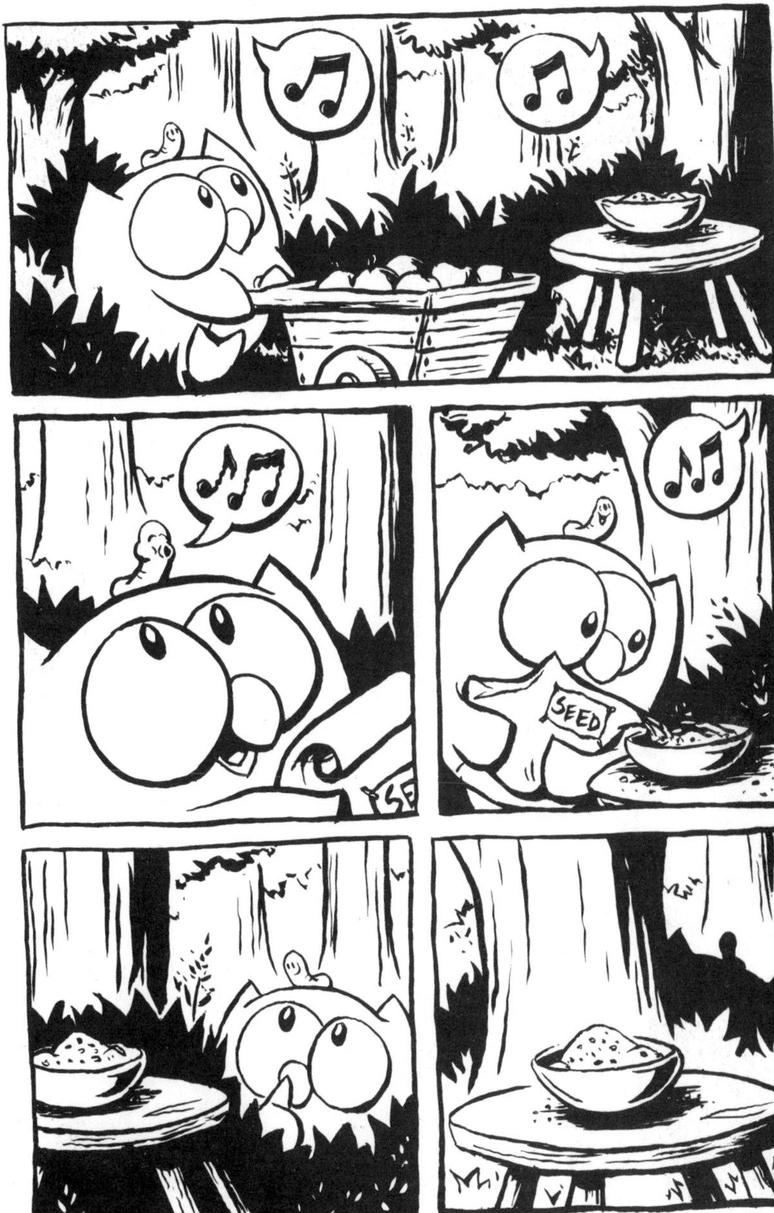
SEED

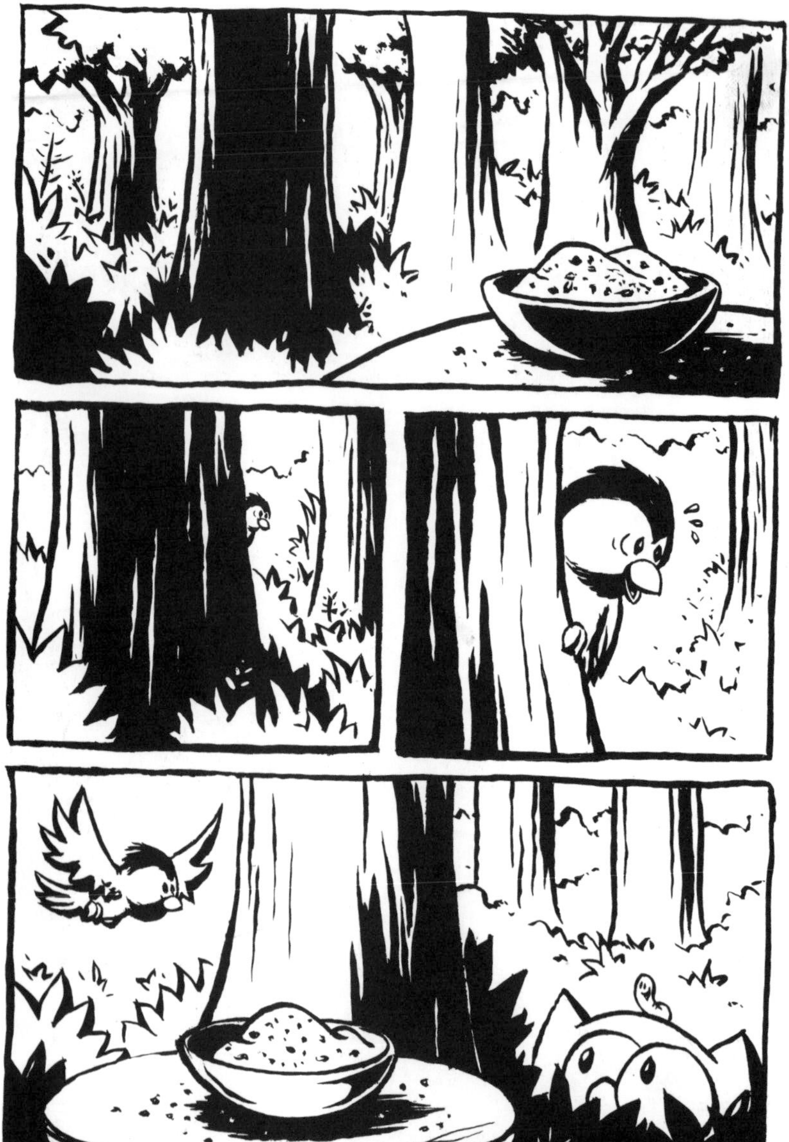

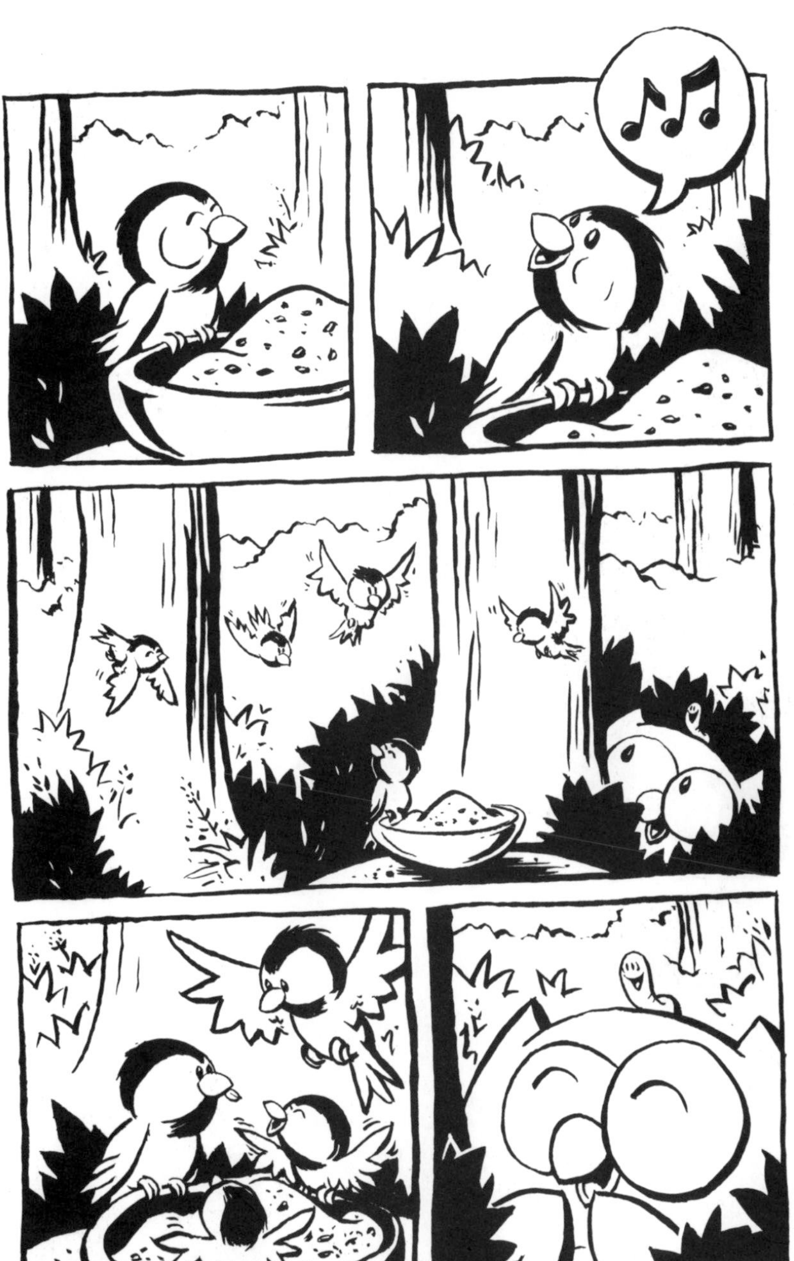

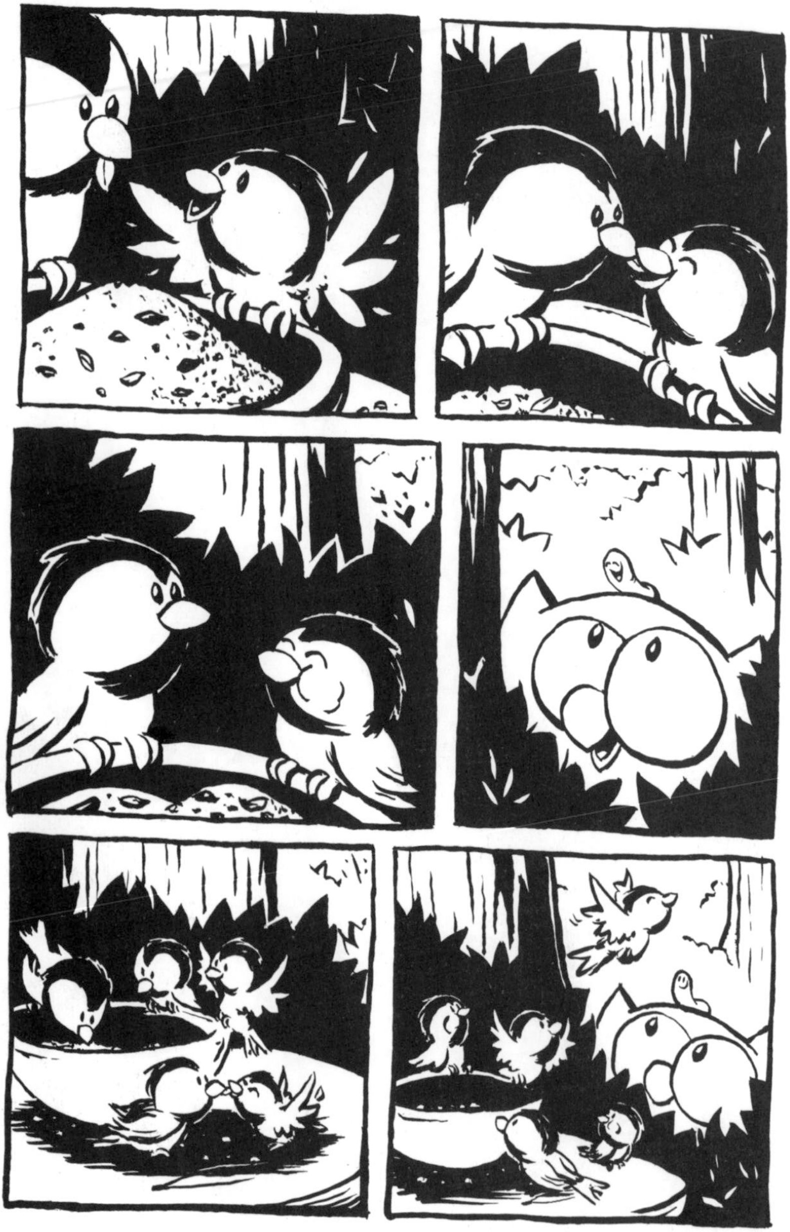

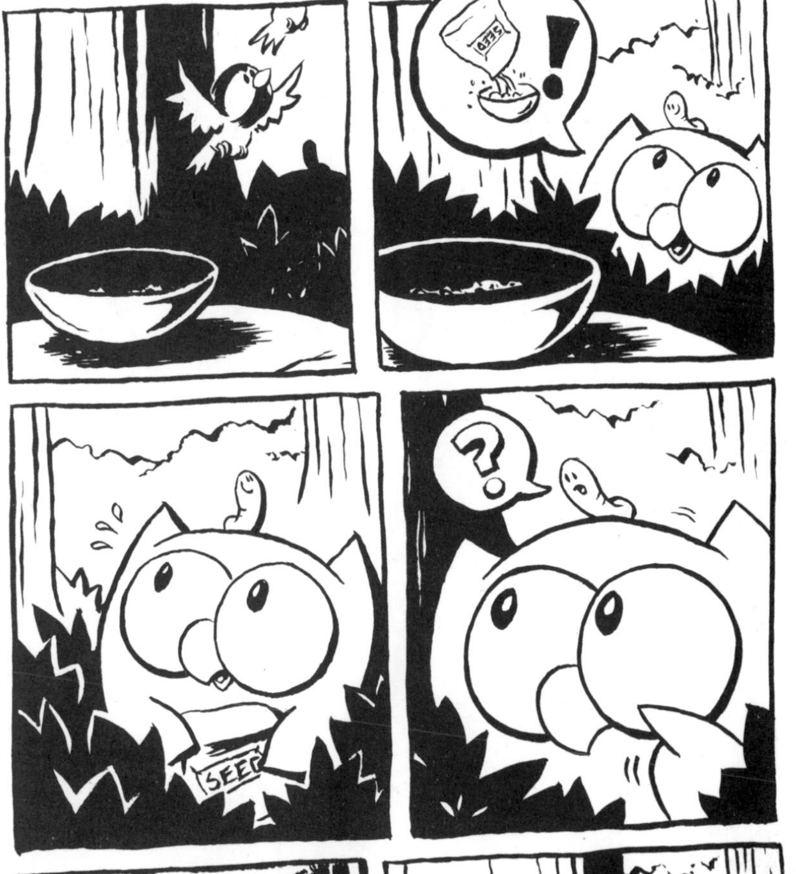
SEED
!
?

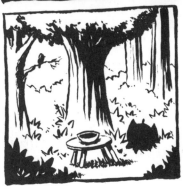

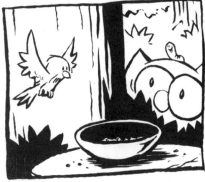

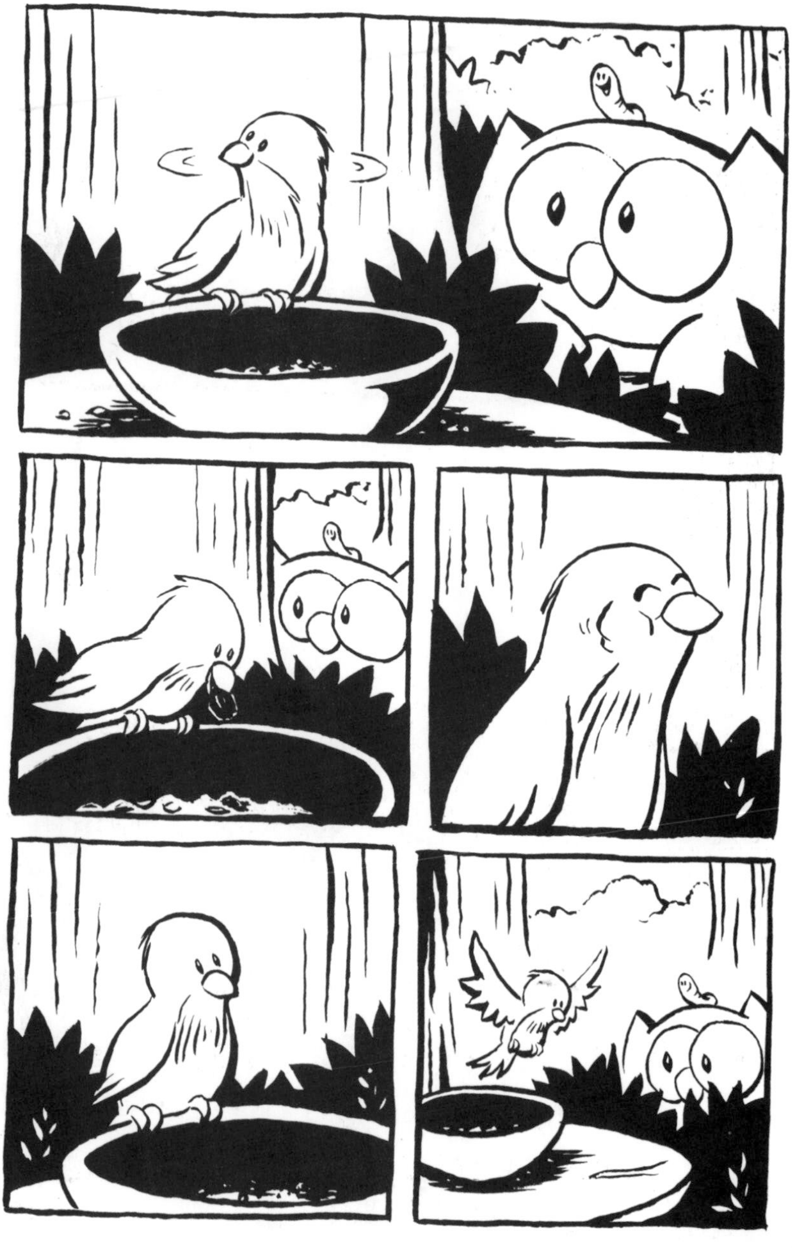

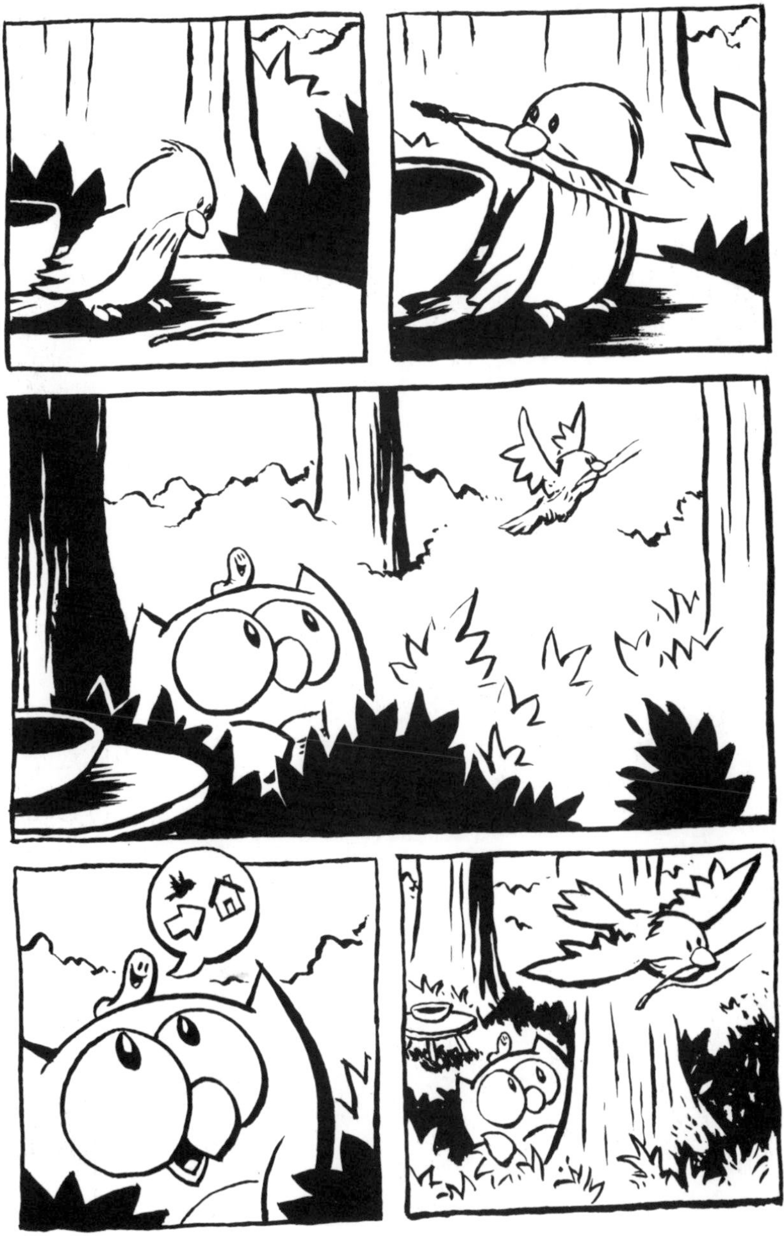

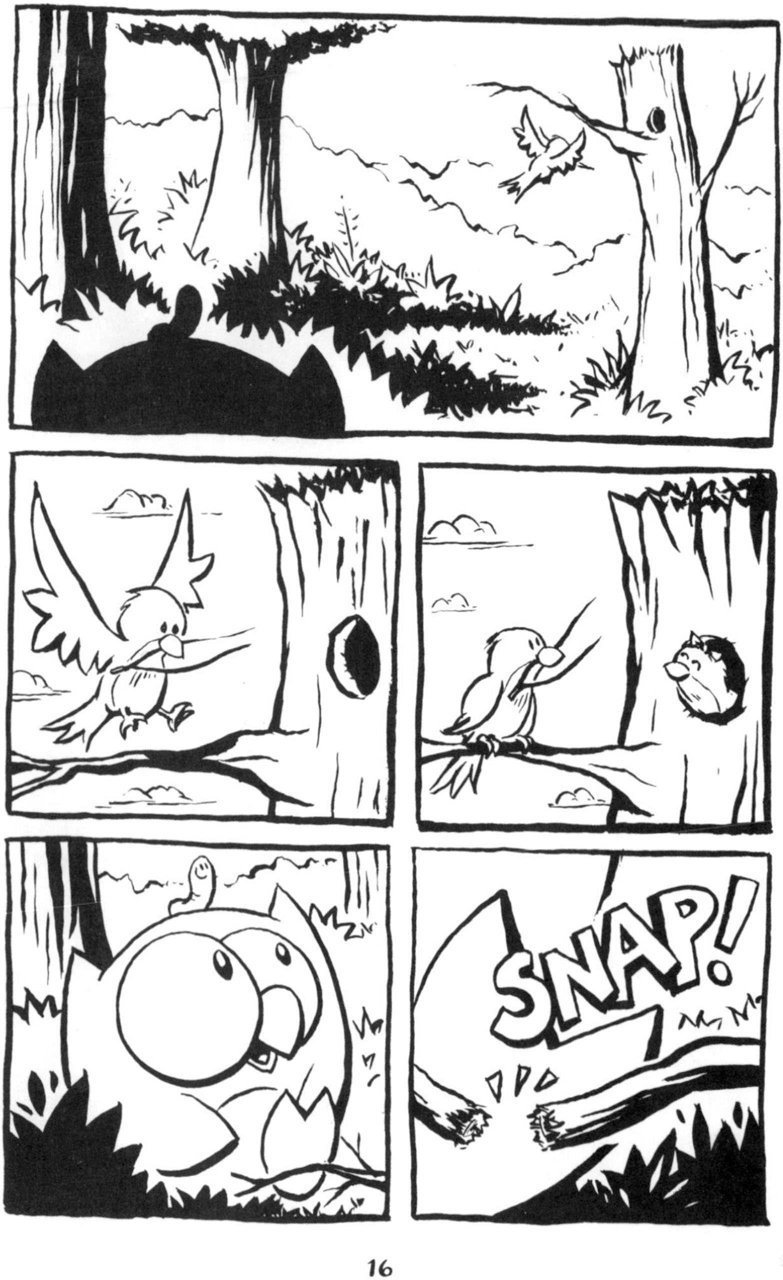
SNAP!

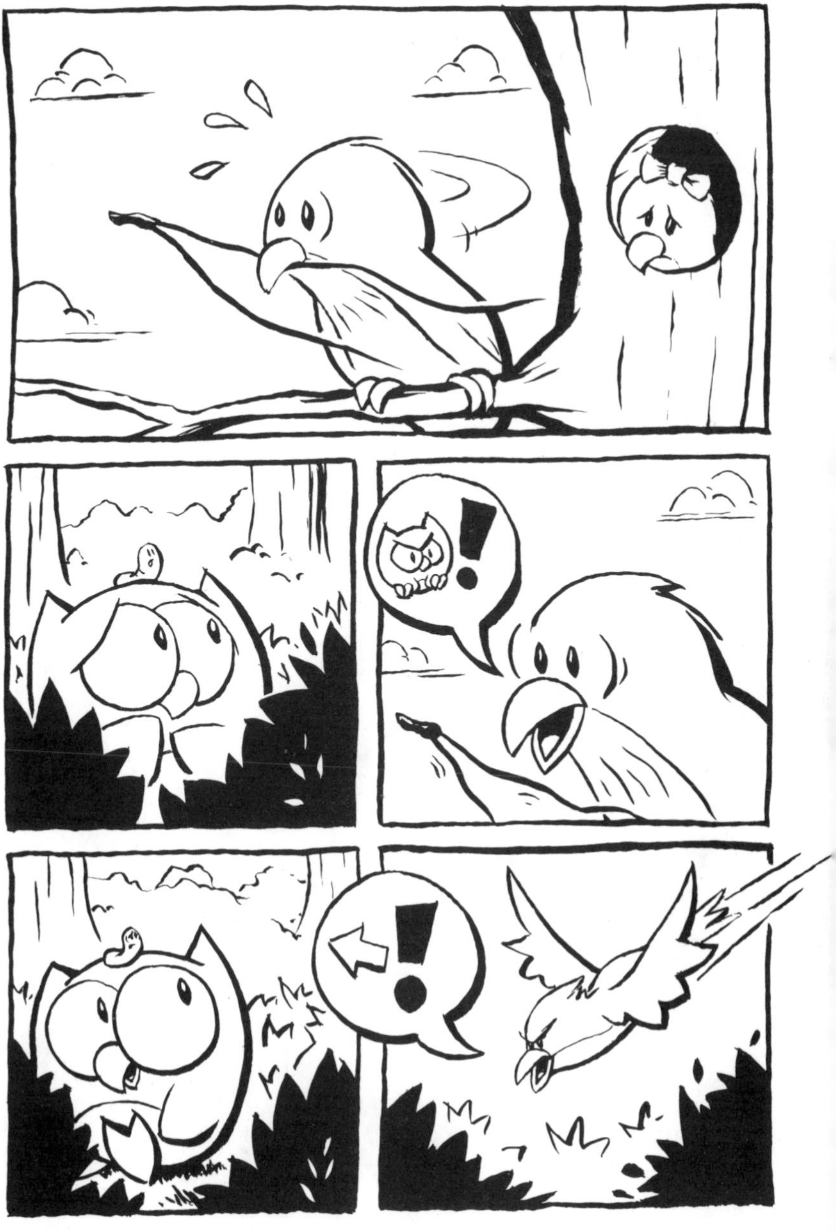
!
!

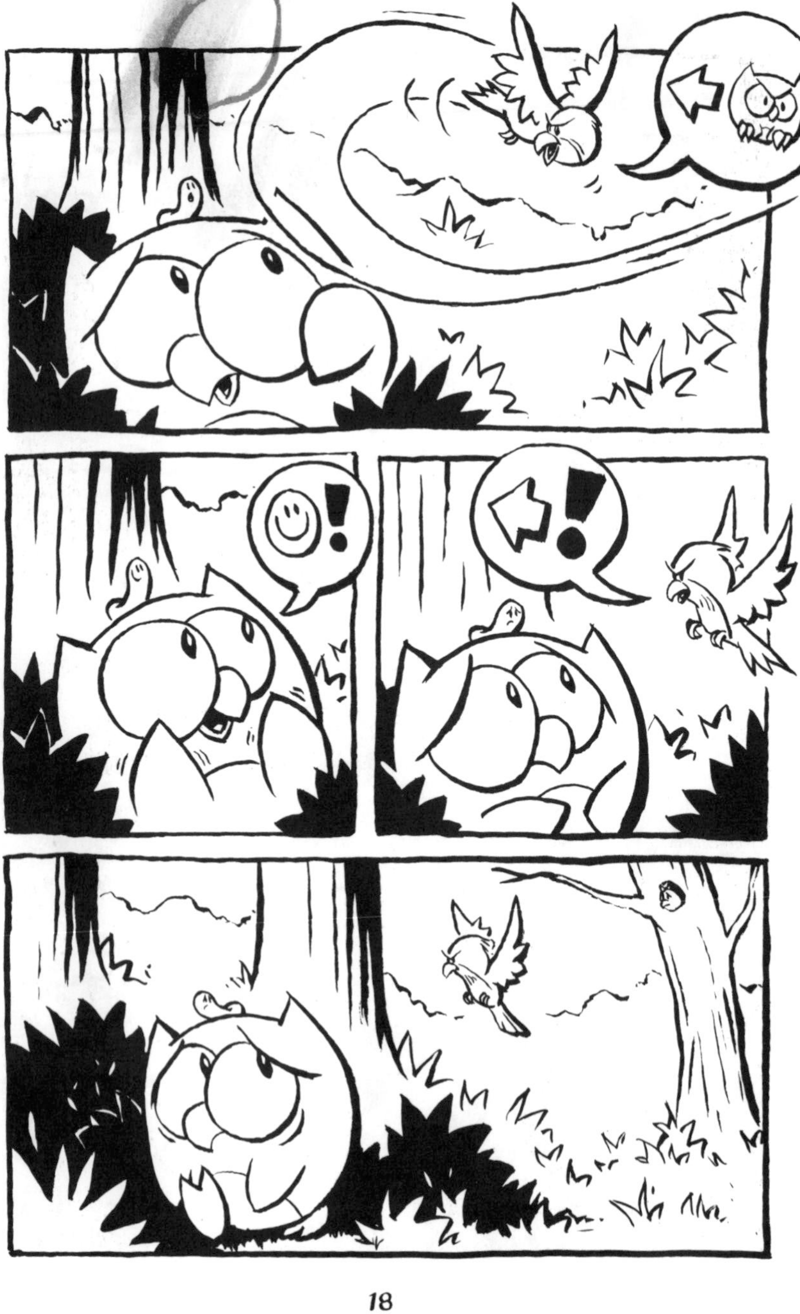

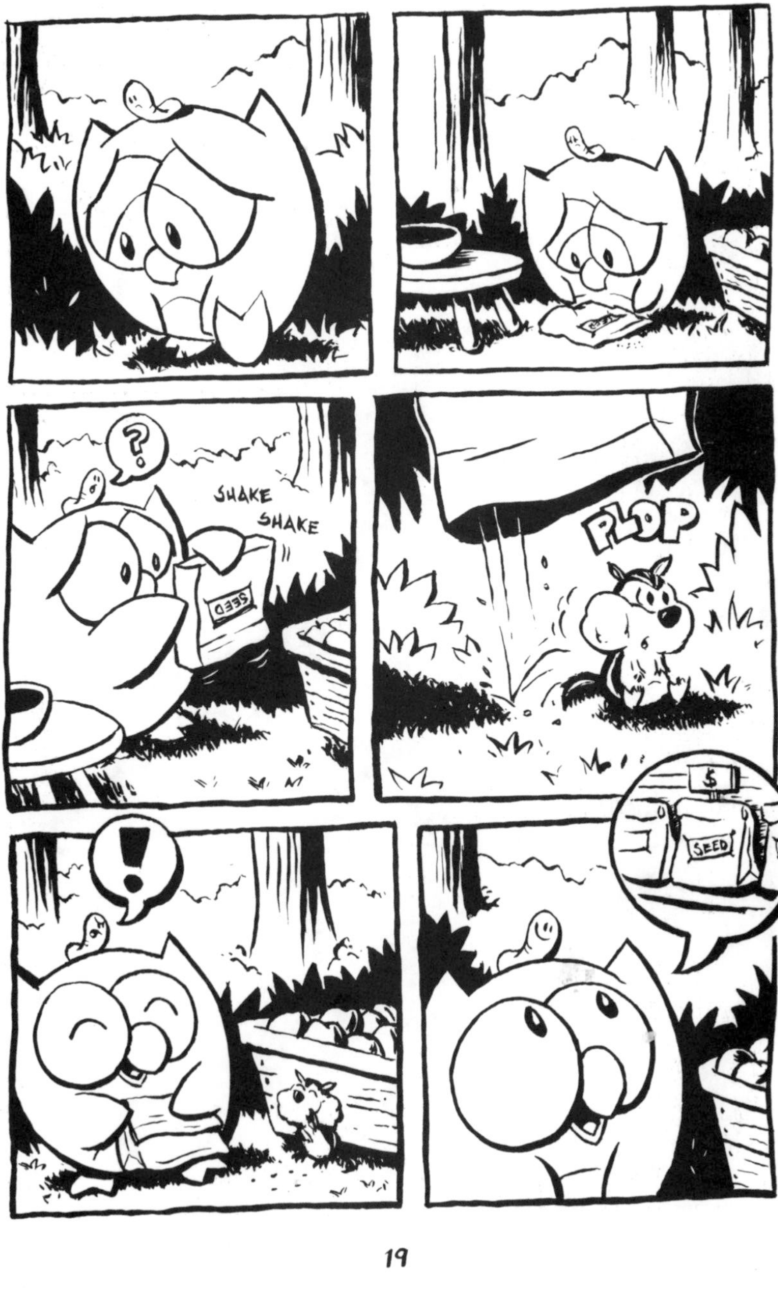
?
SHAKE
SHAKE
SEED
PLOP
!
$
SEED

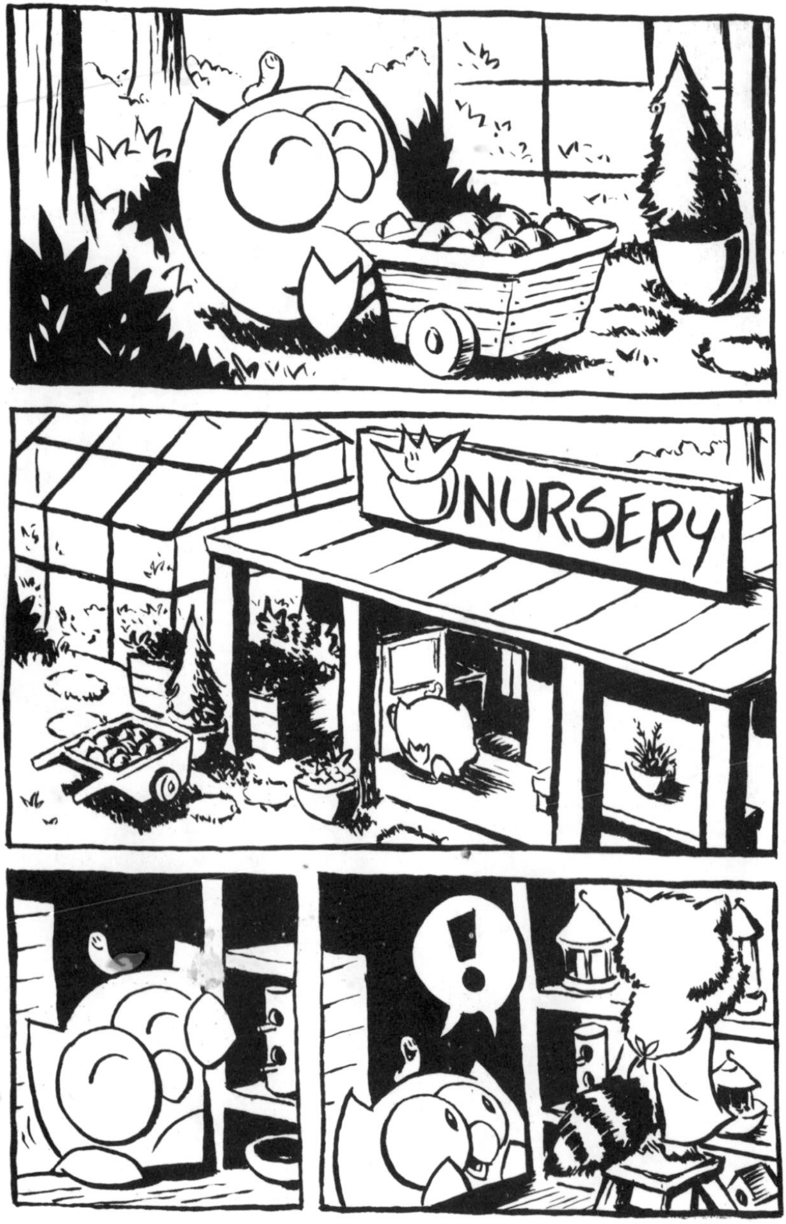
NURSERY
!

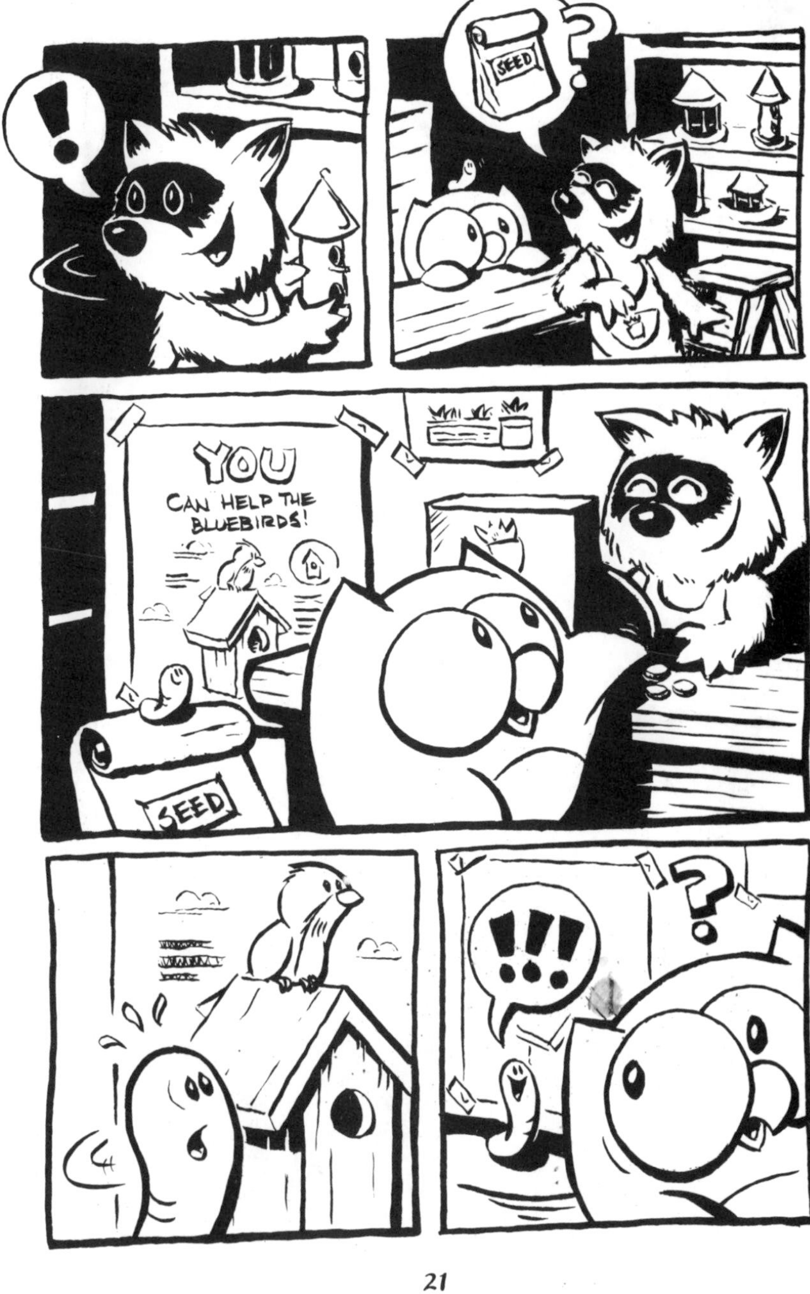
!
SEED
?
YOU
CAN HELP THE BLUEBIRDS!
SEED
!!!
?

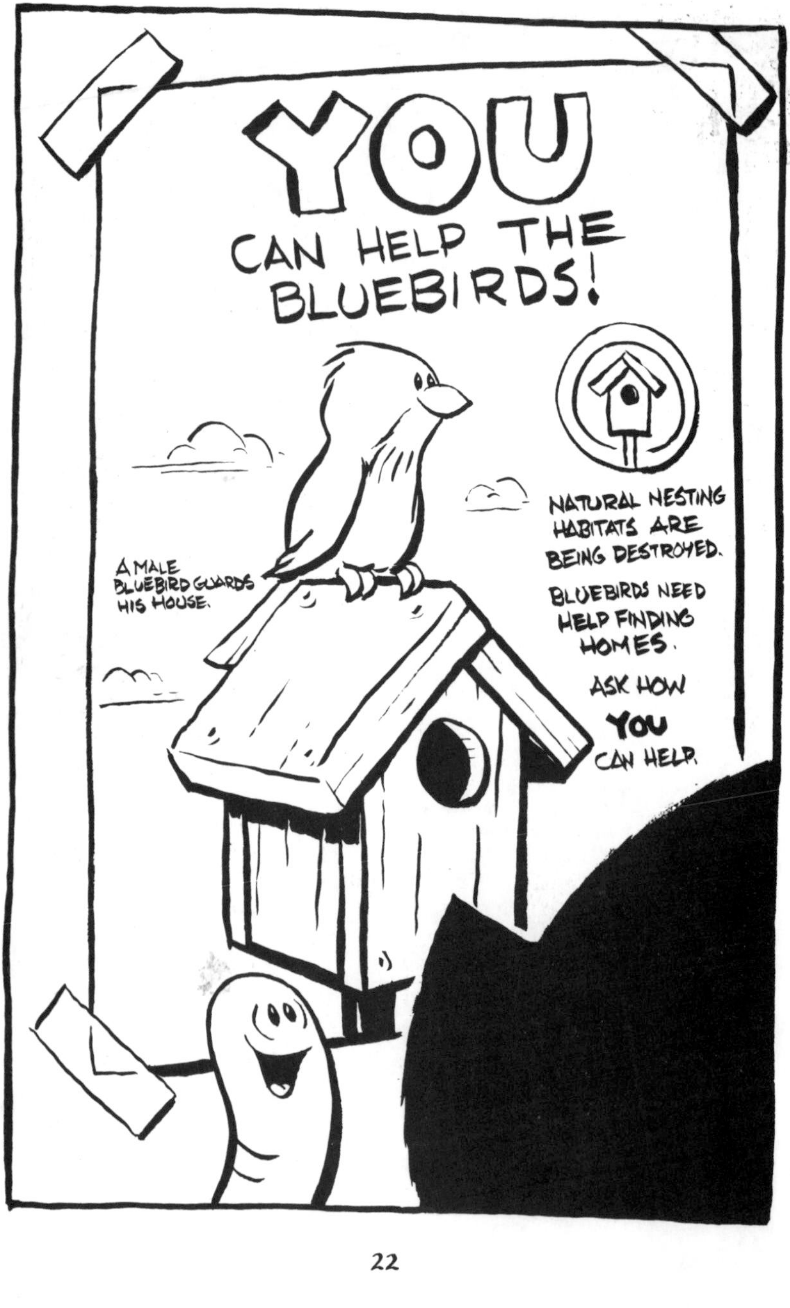

YOU
CAN HELP THE BLUEBIRDS!
A MALE BLUEBIRD GUARDS HIS HOUSE.
NATURAL NESTING HABITATS ARE BEING DESTROYED.
BLUEBIRDS NEED HELP FINDING HOMES.
ASK HOW YOU CAN HELP.

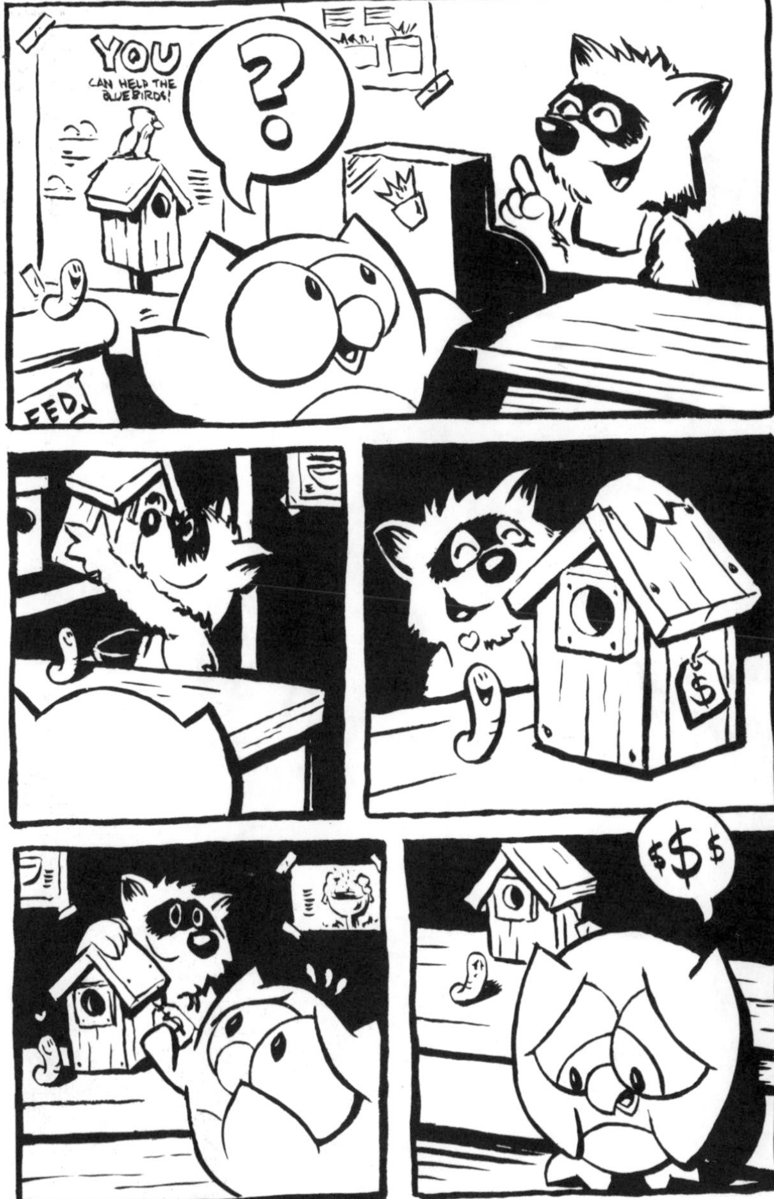
YOU
CAN HELP THE BLUEBIRDS!
?
FED
$$$

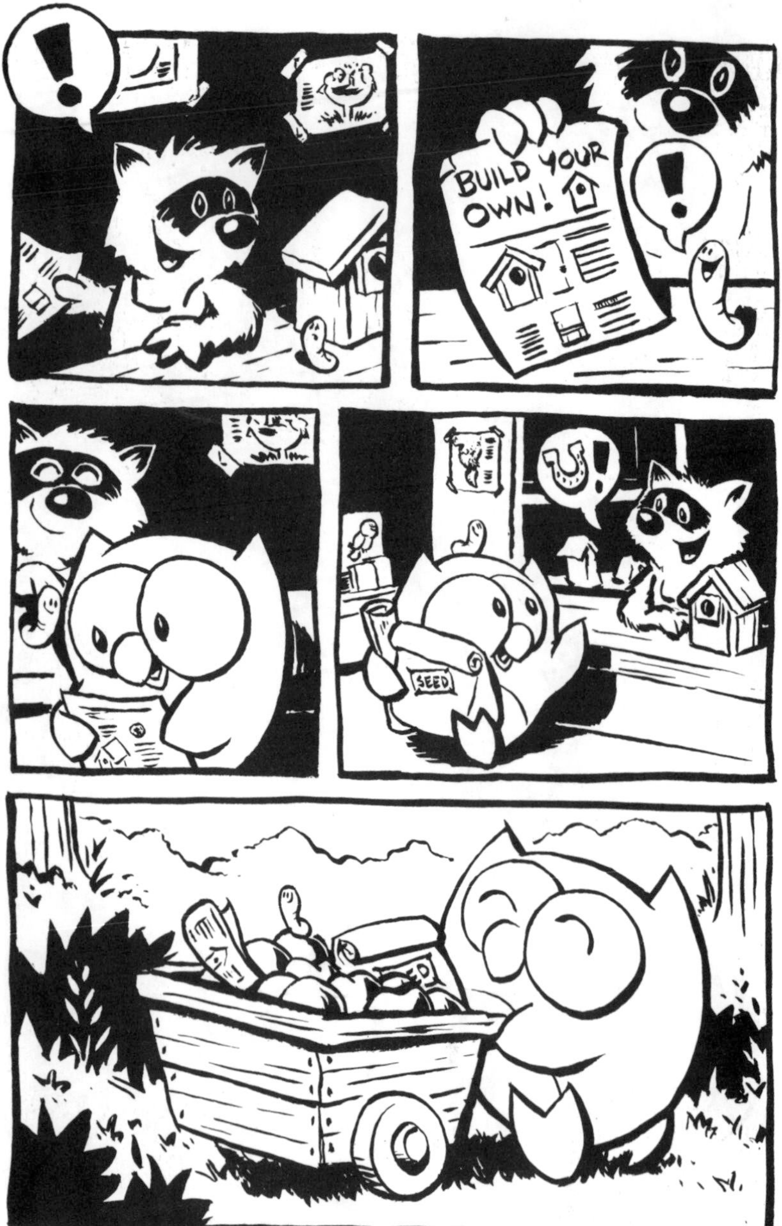
!
BUILD YOUR OWN!
!
SEED
!

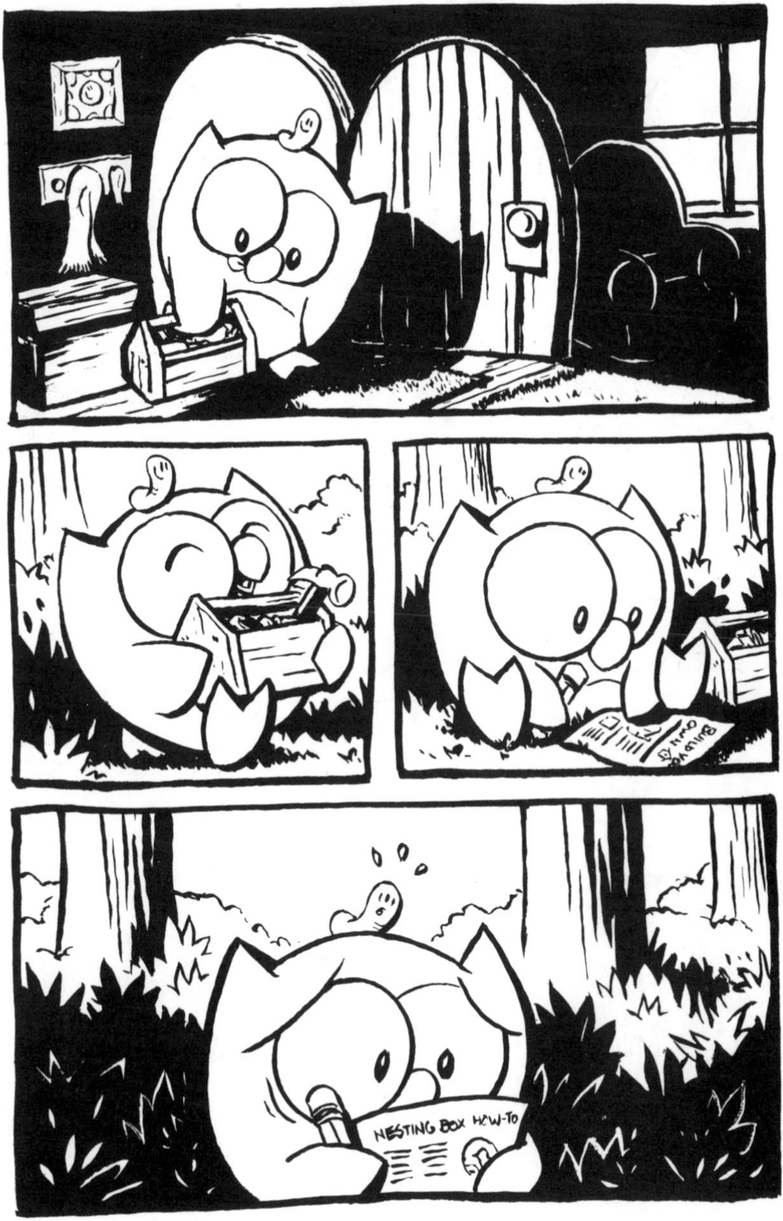
NESTING BOX HOW-TO

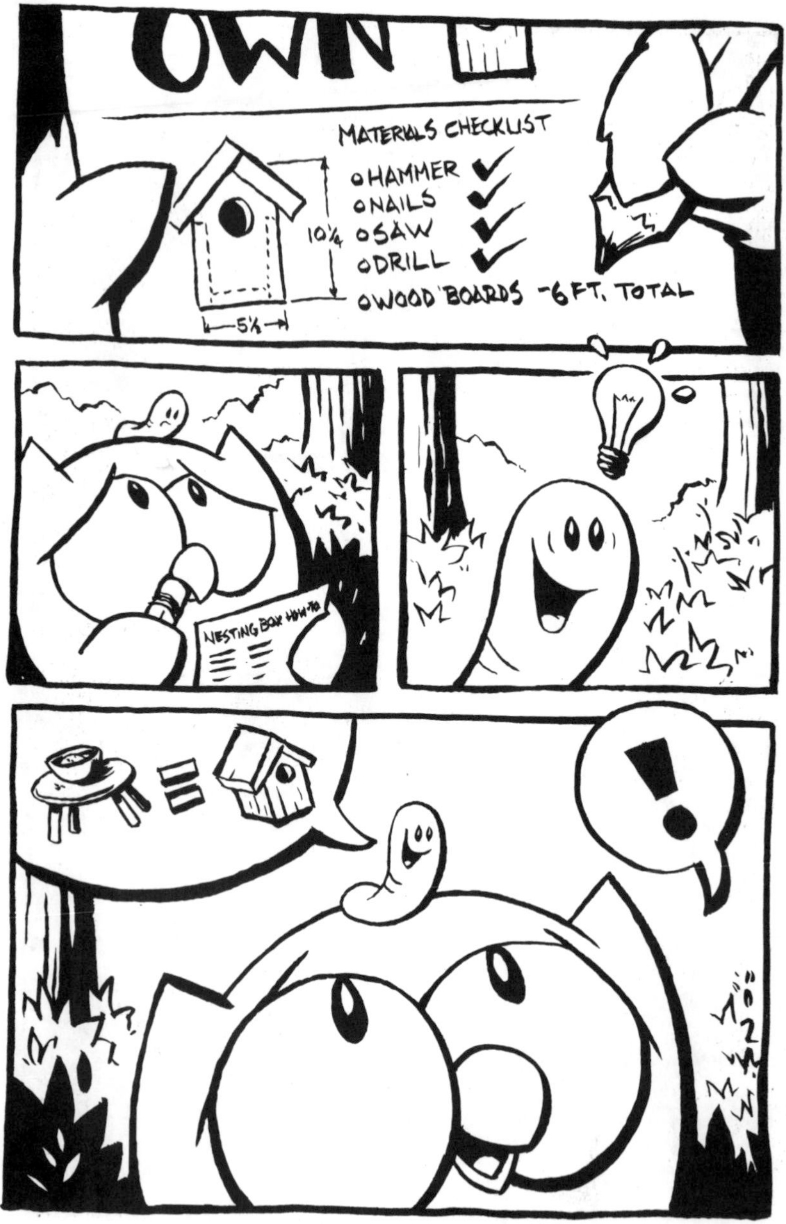
OWN
MATERIALS CHECKLIST
HAMMER
NAILS
SAW
DRILL
WOOD BOARDS -6 FT. TOTAL
10¼
5½
NESTING BOX HOW-TO
!

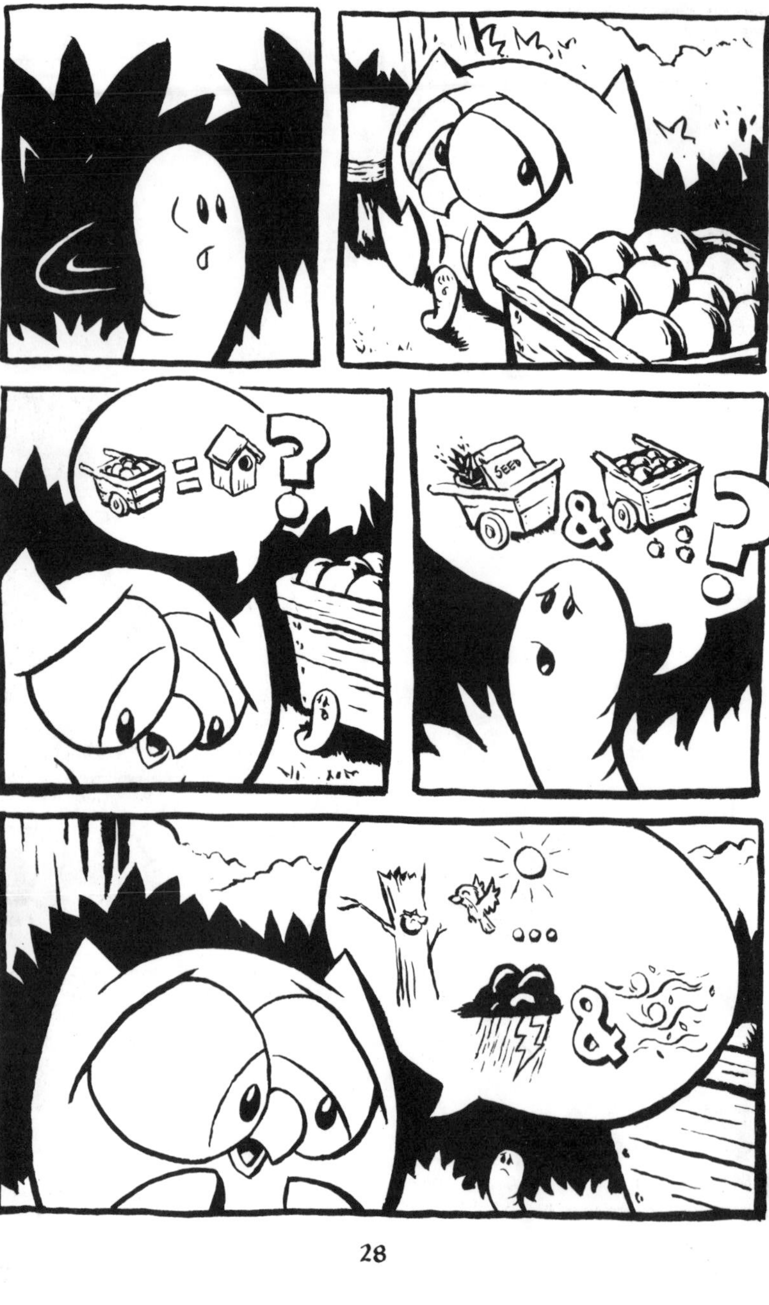
SEED
&
&

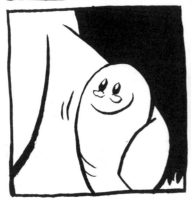

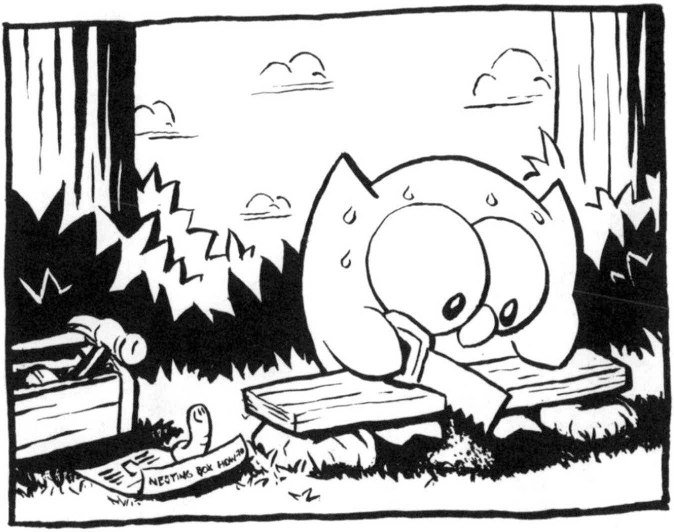
NESTING BOX HOW-TO

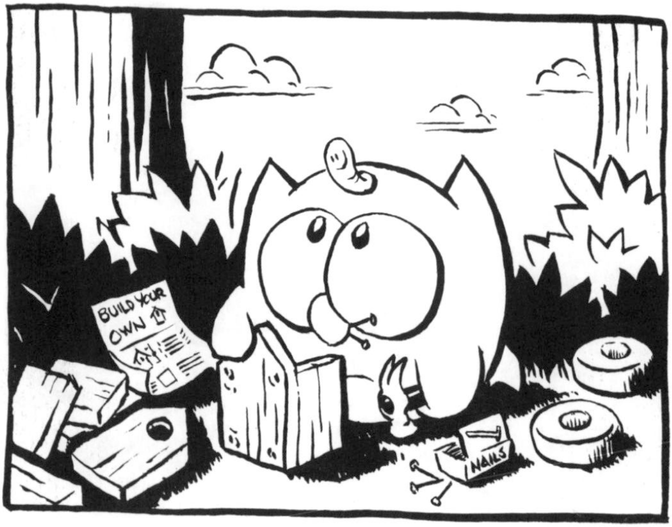
BUILD YOUR OWN
NAILS

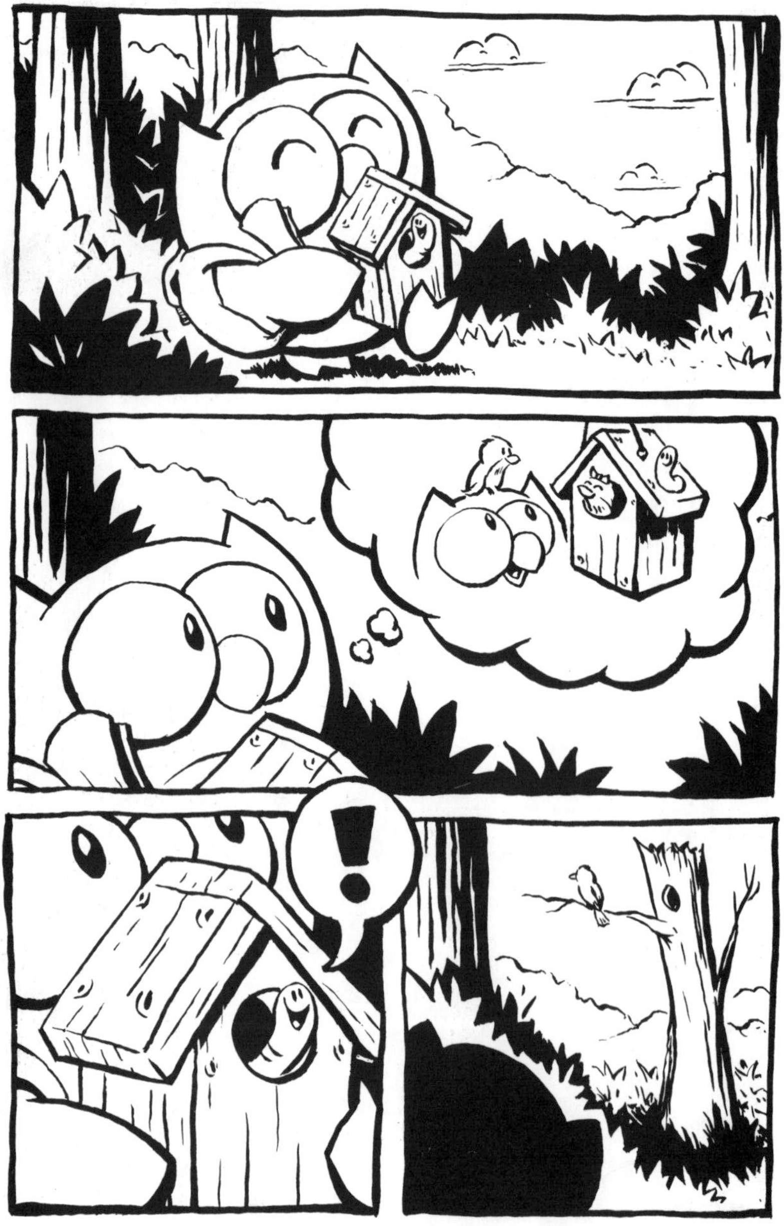
!

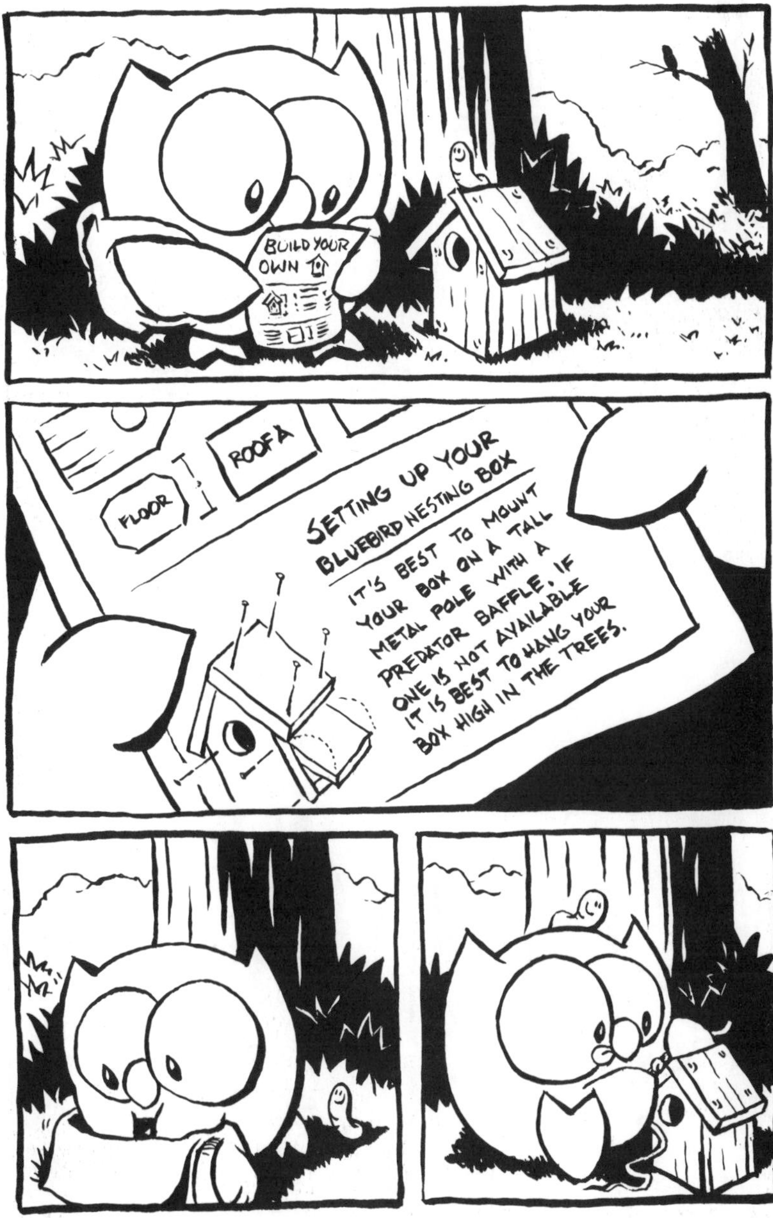
BUILD YOUR OWN
ROOF A
FLOOR
SETTING UP YOUR BLUEBIRD NESTING BOX
IT'S BEST TO MOUNT YOUR BOX ON A TALL METAL POLE WITH A PREDATOR BAFFLE. IF ONE IS NOT AVAILABLE IT IS BEST TO HANG YOUR BOX HIGH IN THE TREES.

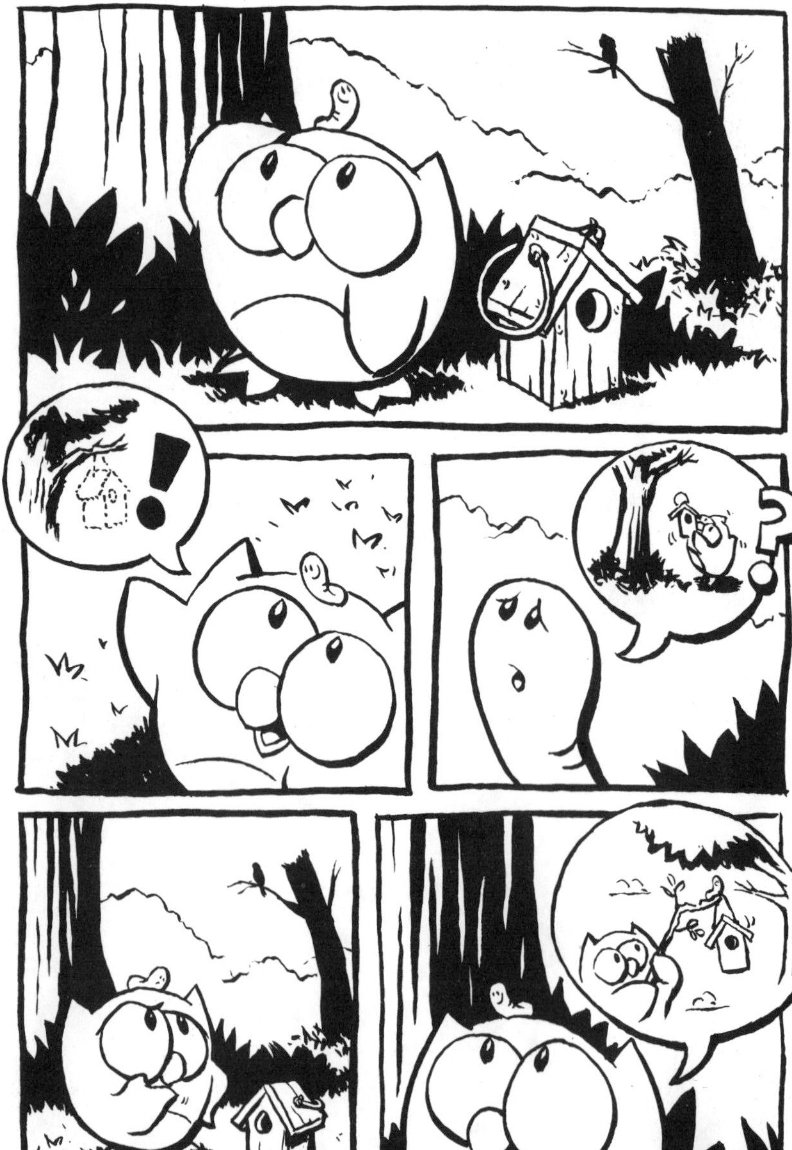
!
?

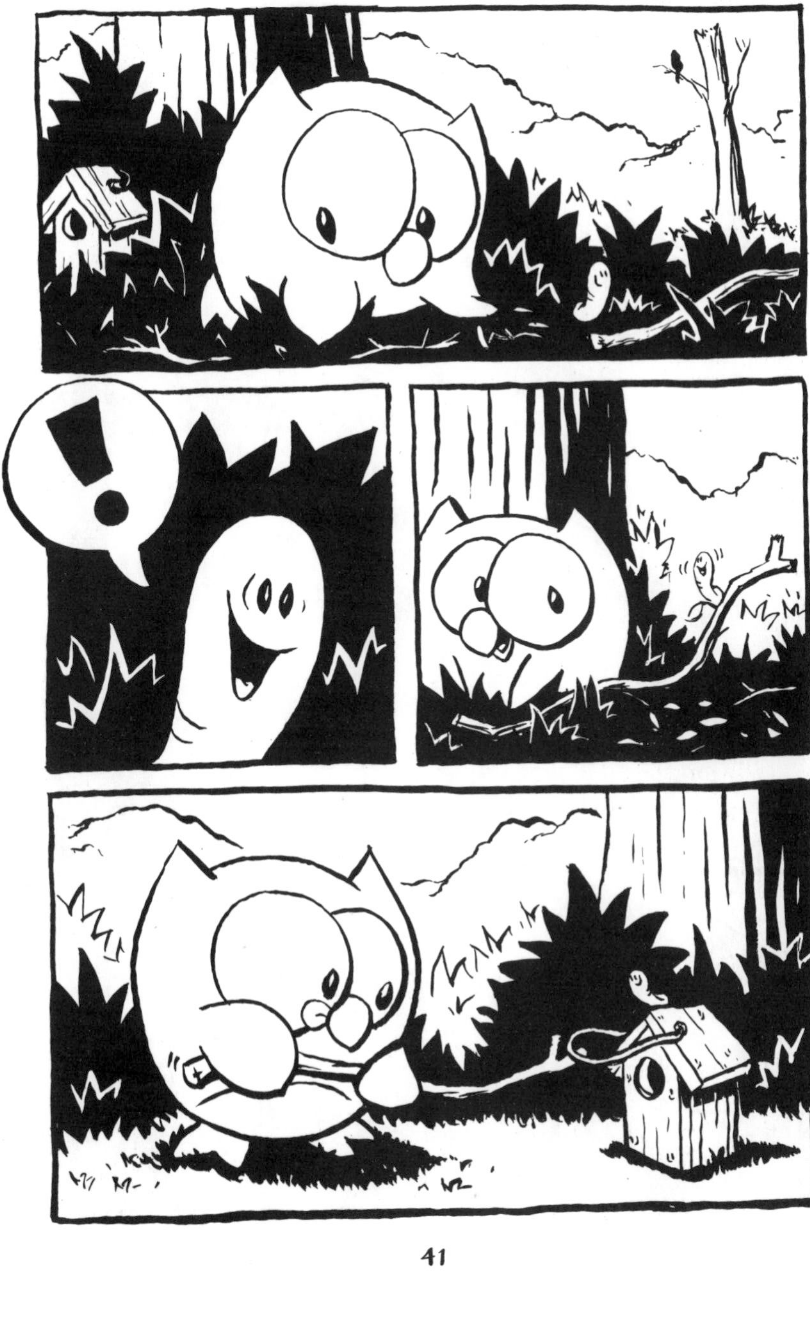
!

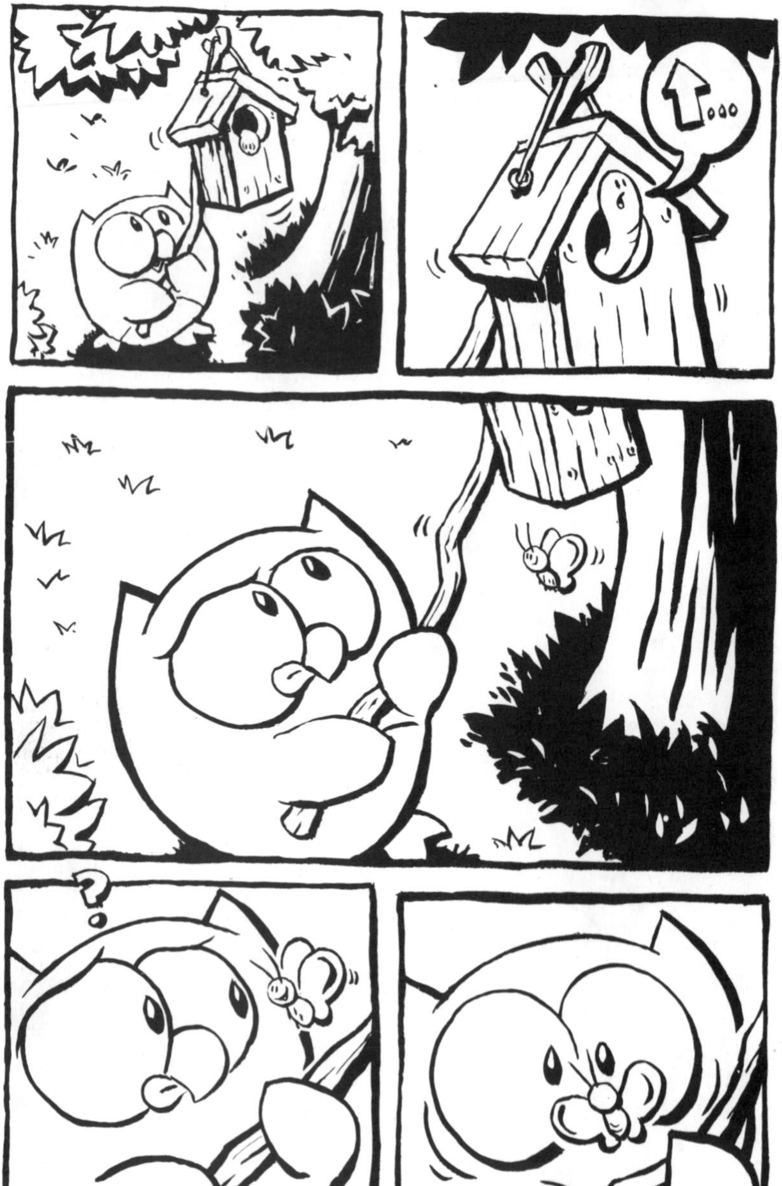

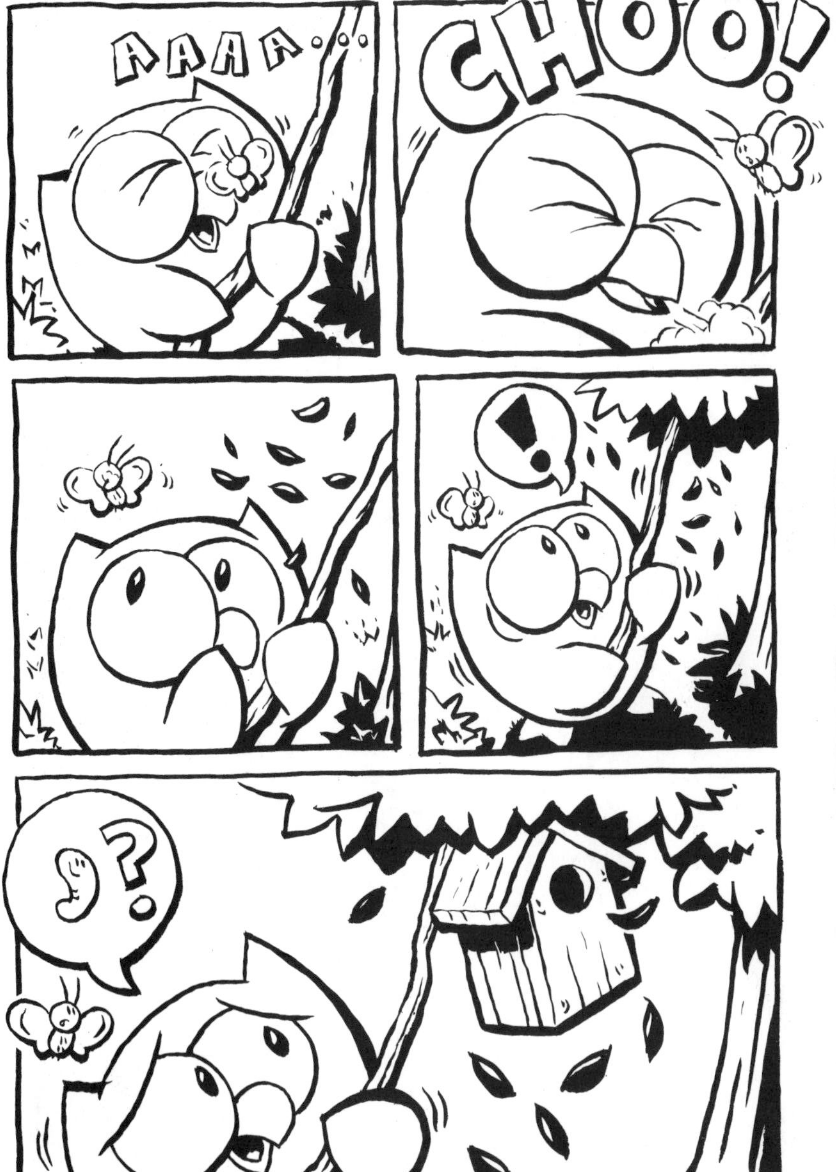
AAAA...
CHOO!
!
?

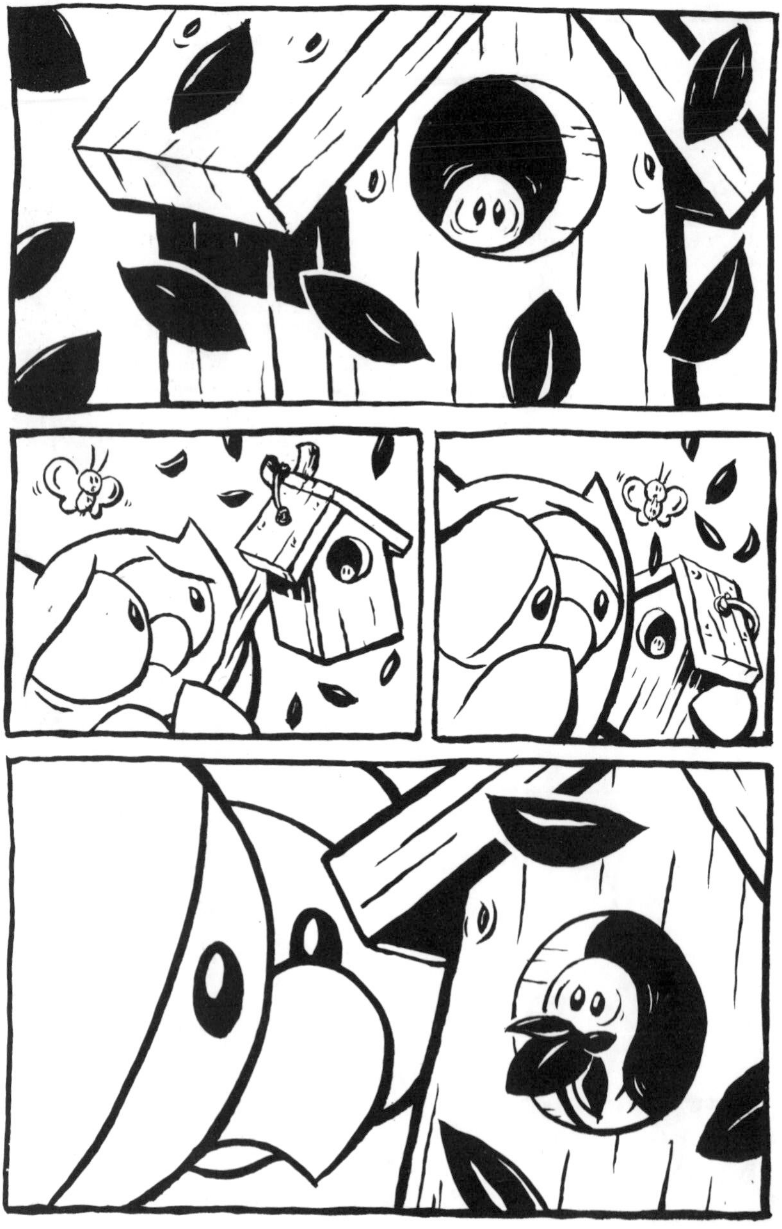

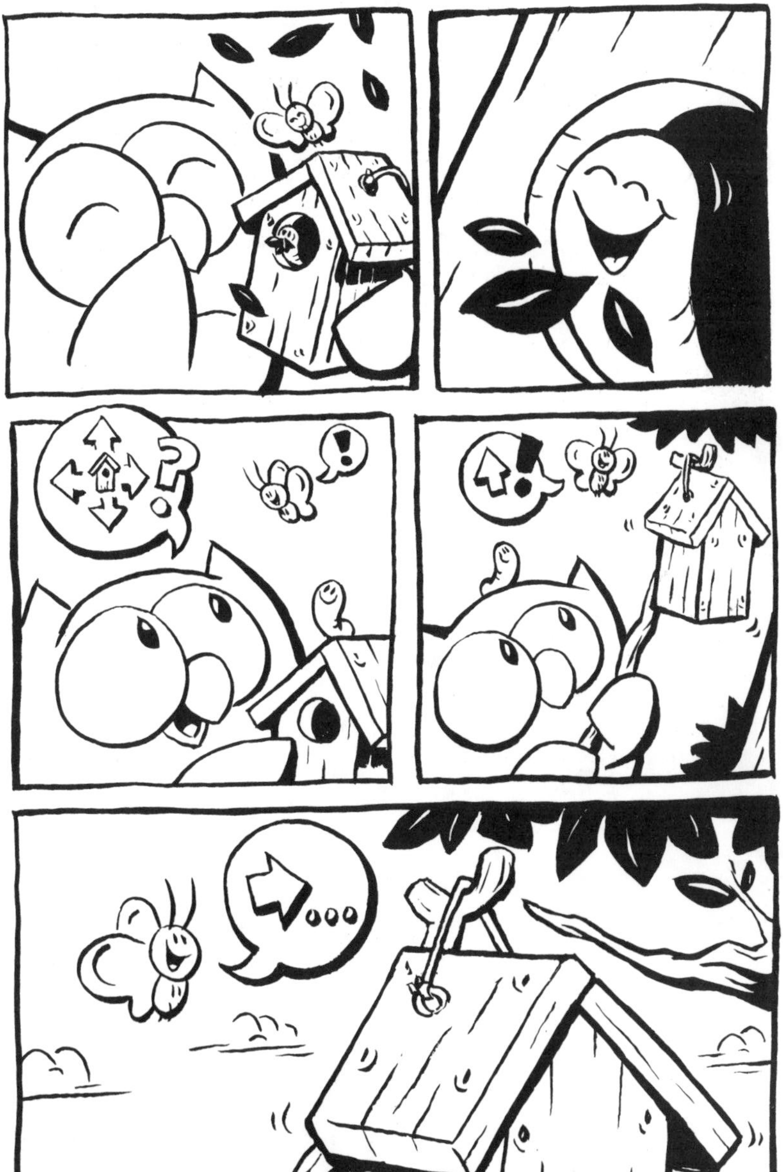

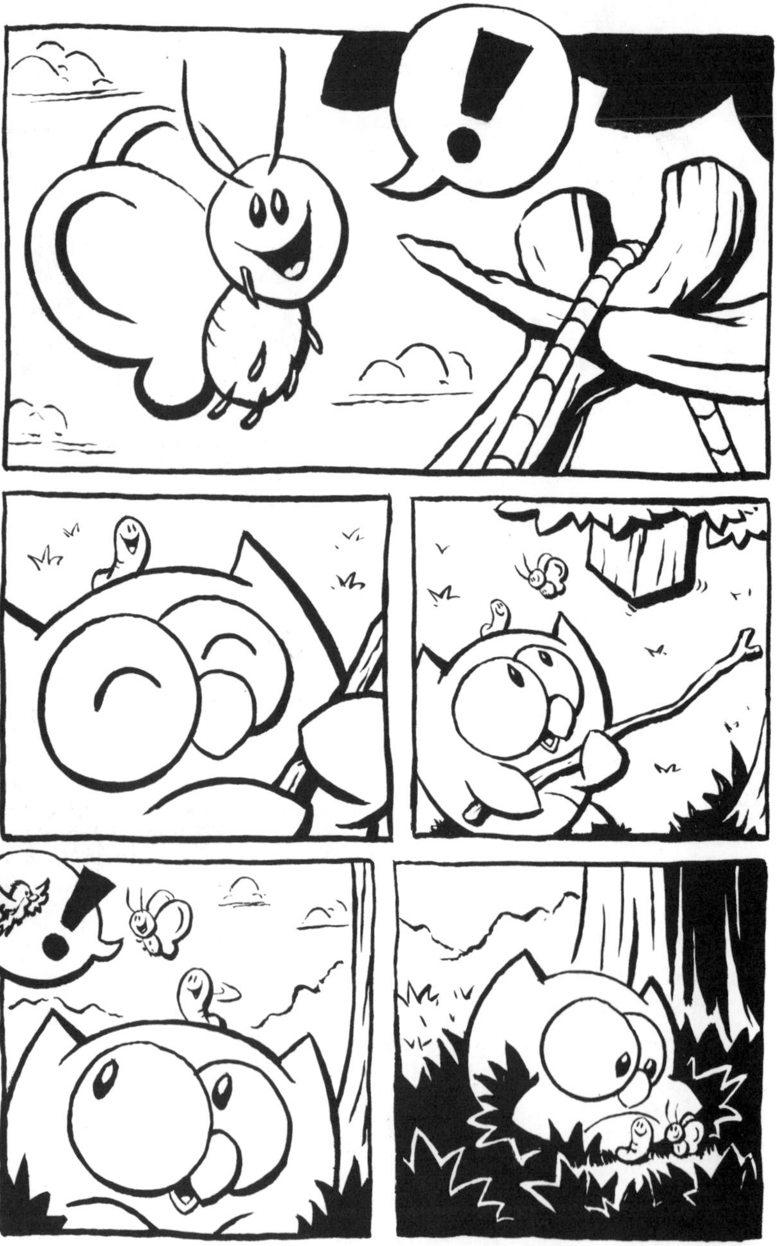
!
!

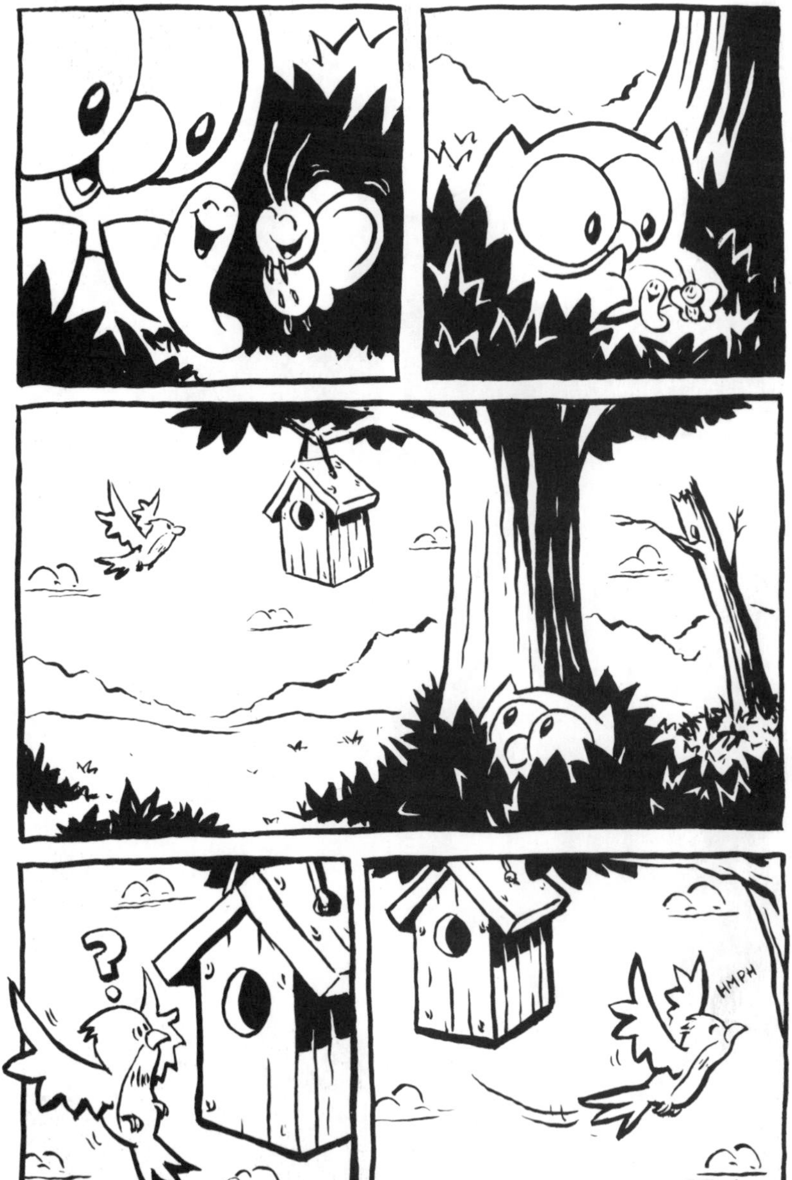
?
HMPH

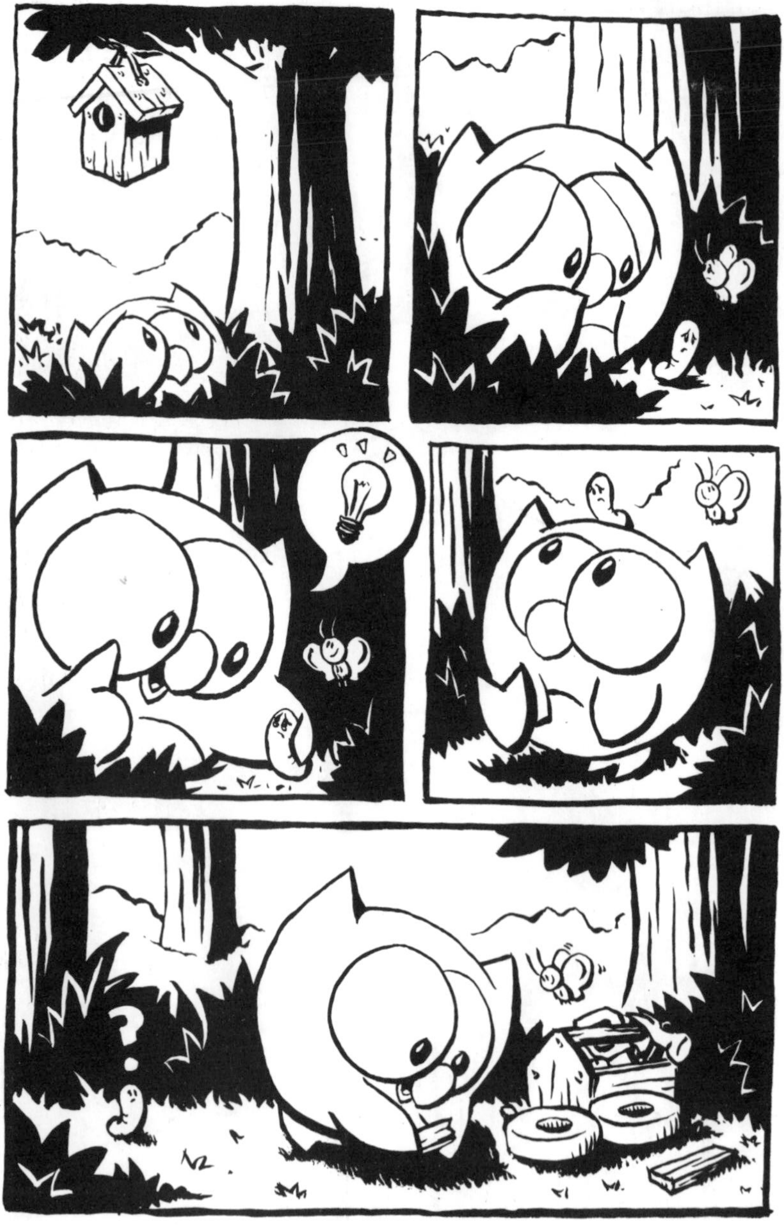
?

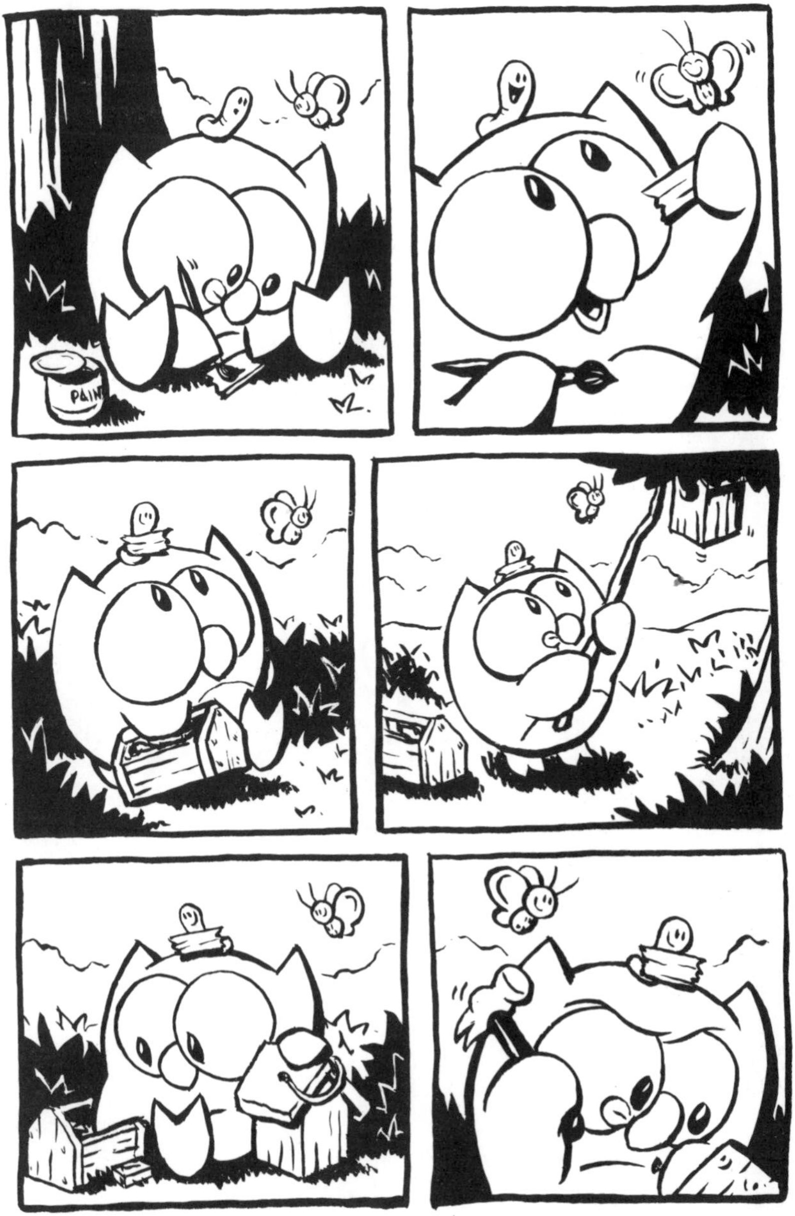

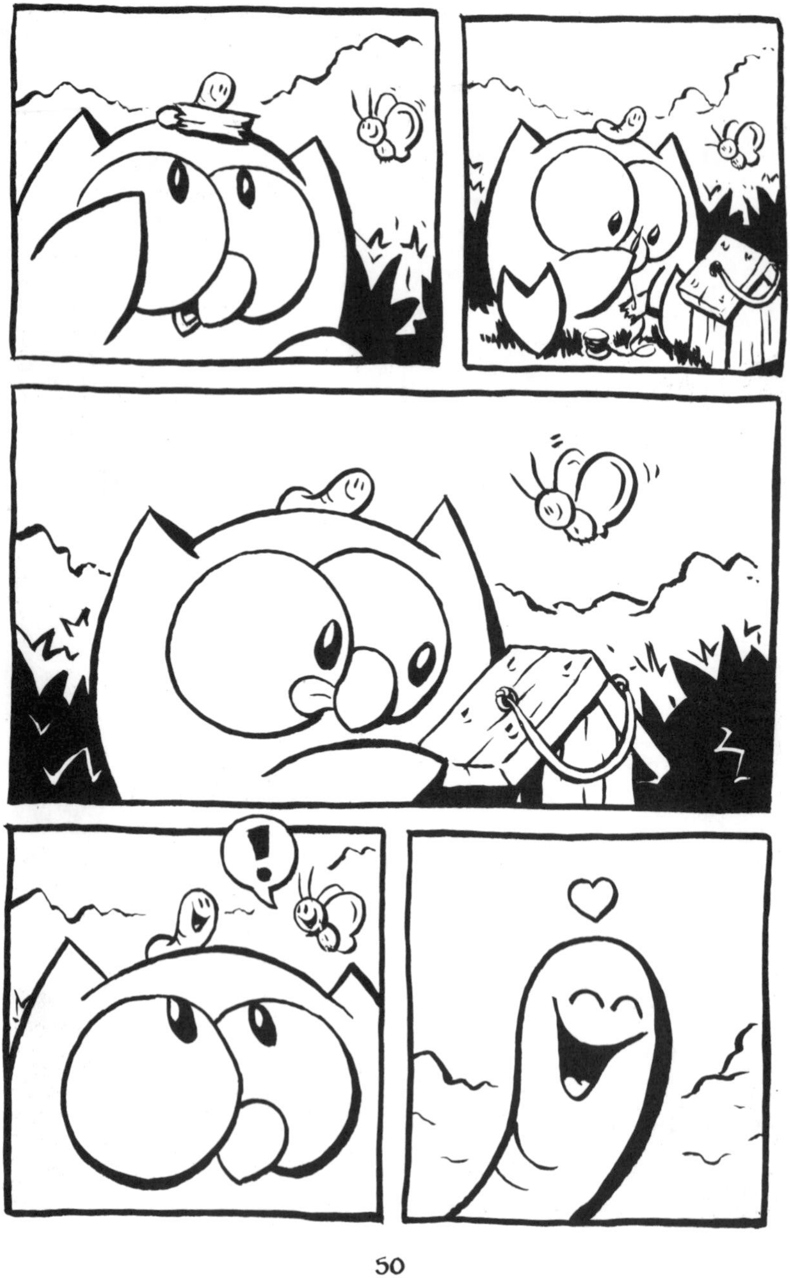
!

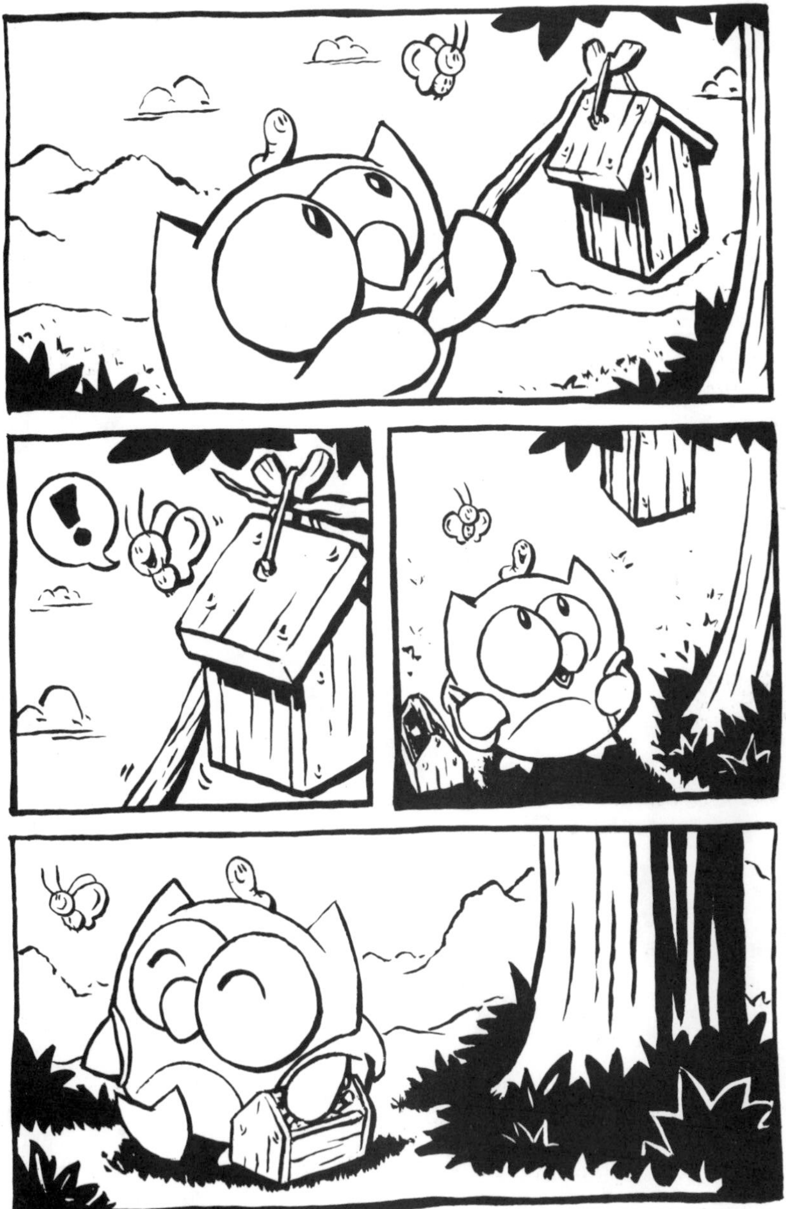
!

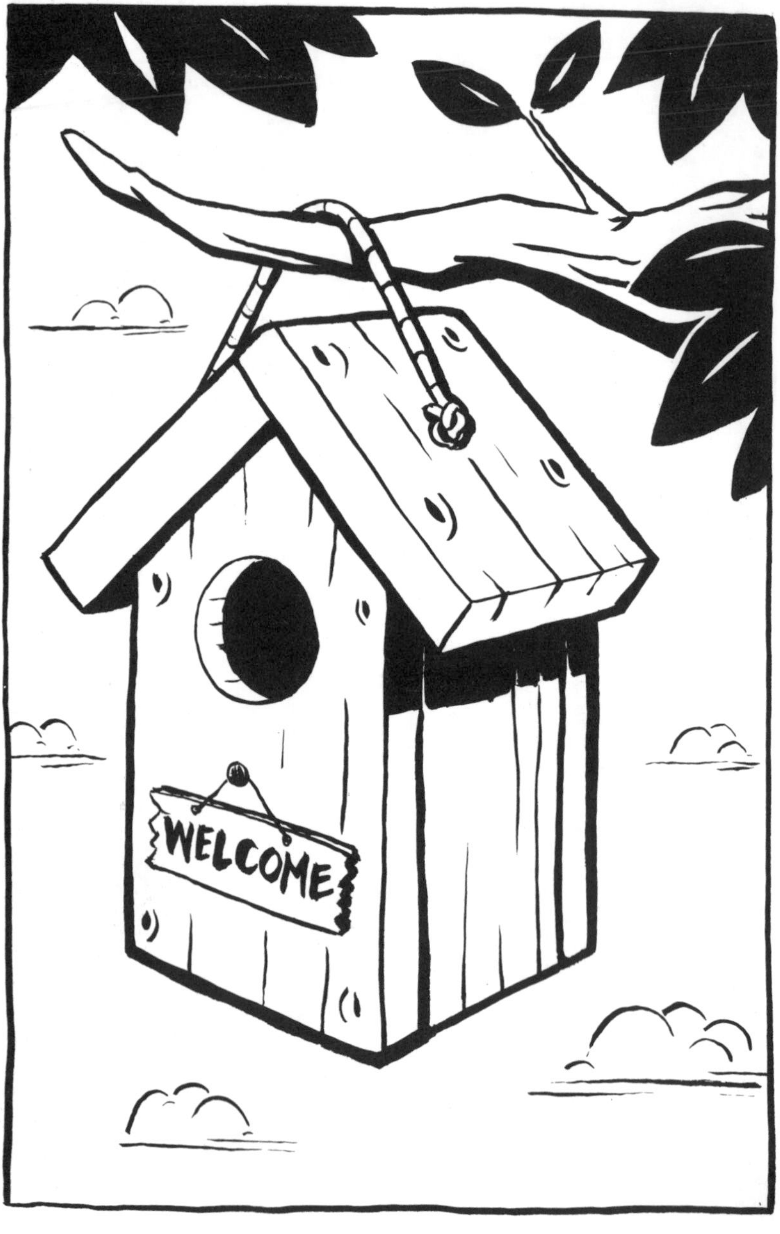
WELCOME

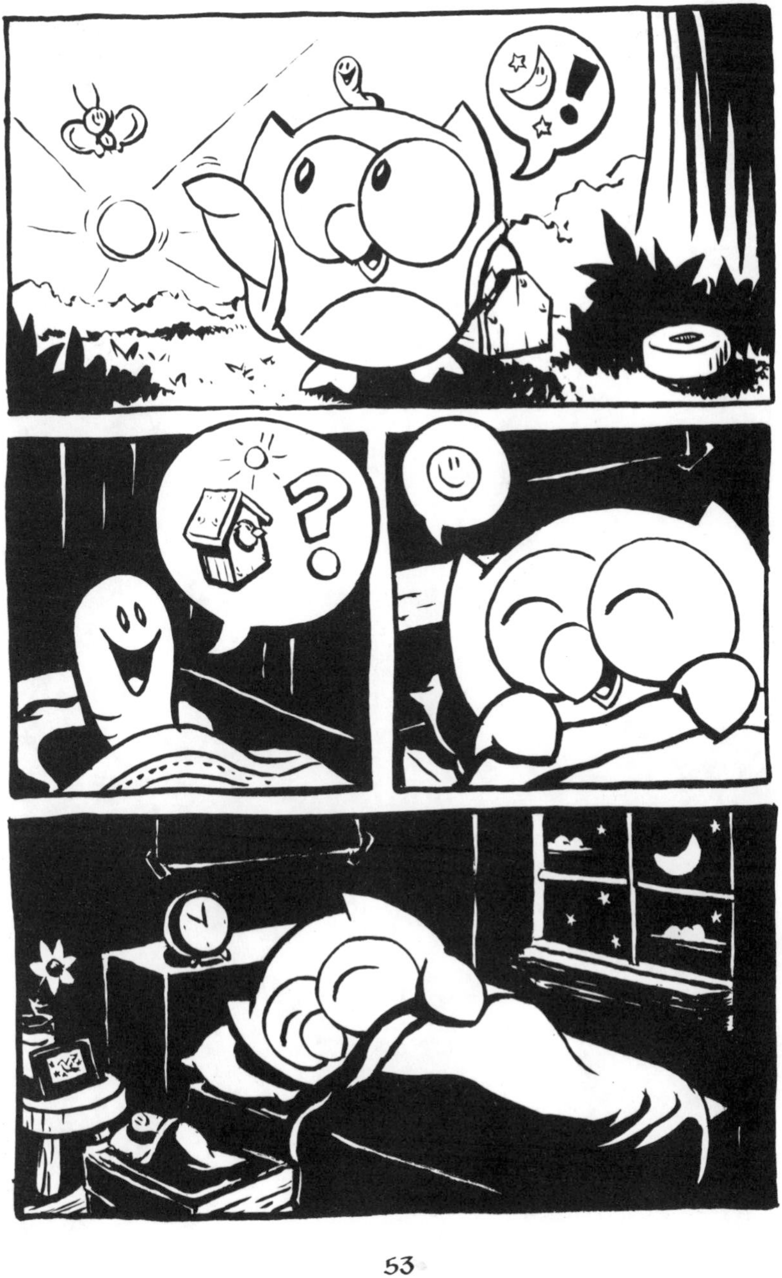

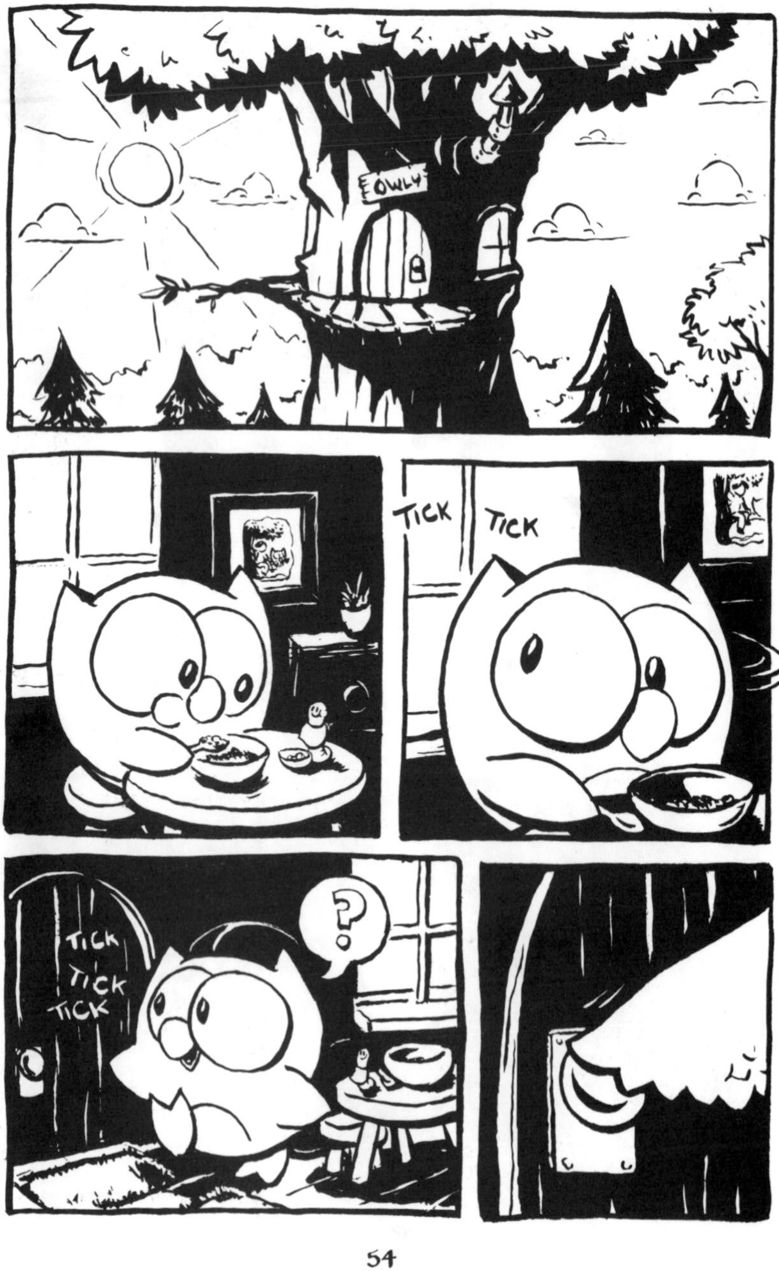
OWLY
TICK
TICK
?
TICK
TICK
TICK

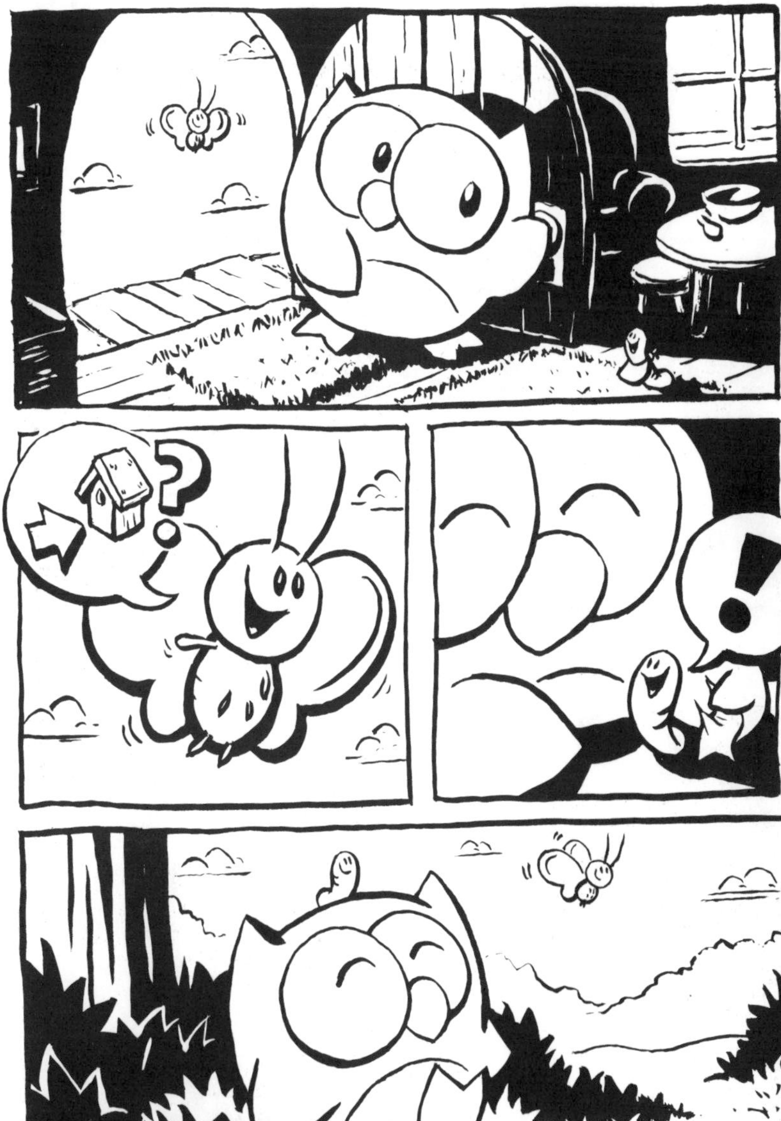
?
!

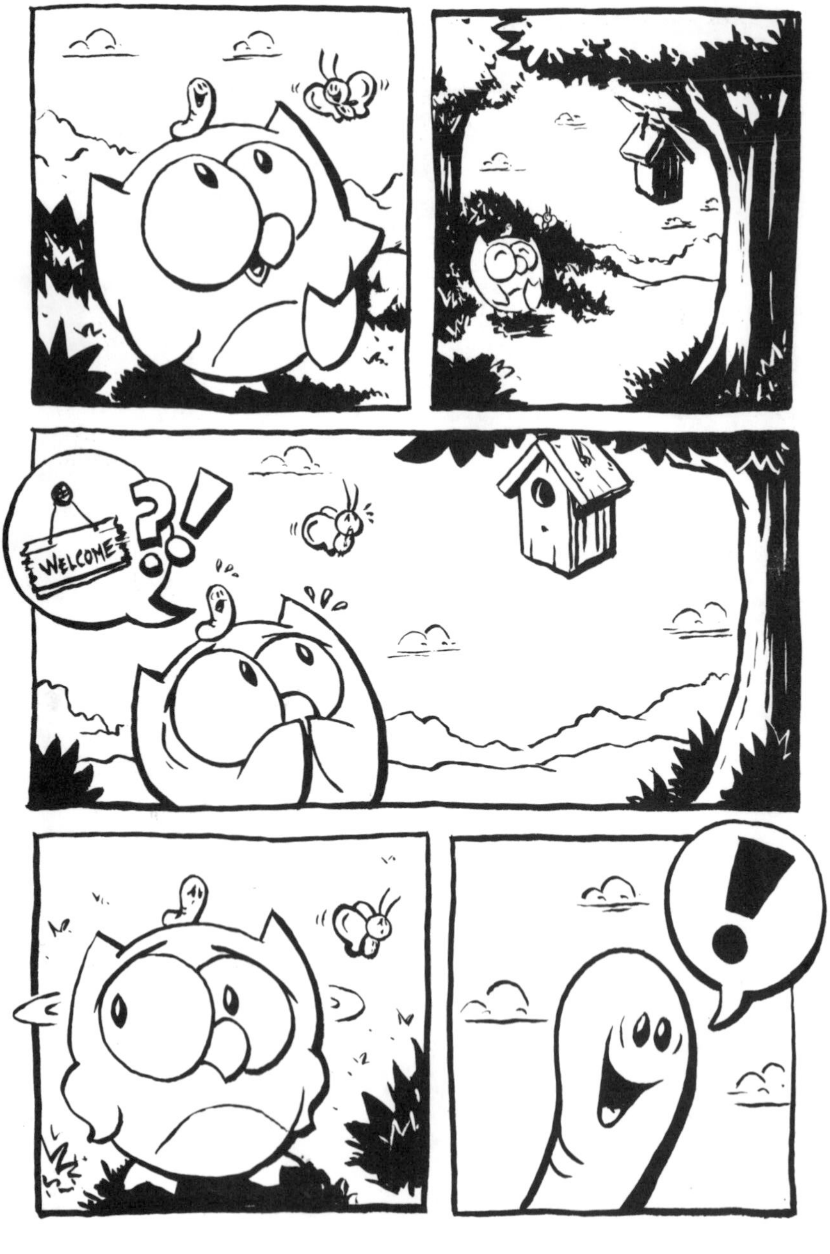
WELCOME
?!
!

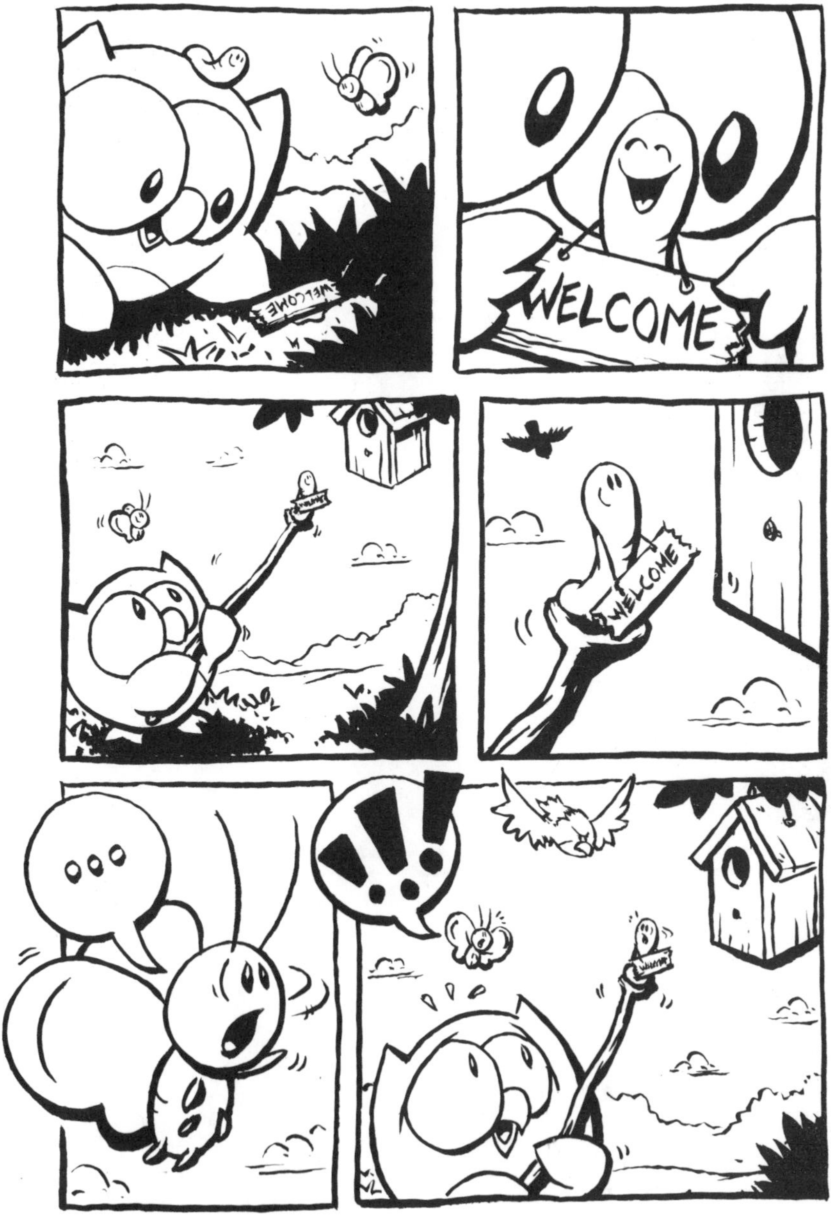
WELCOME
WELCOME
WELCOME
...
!!

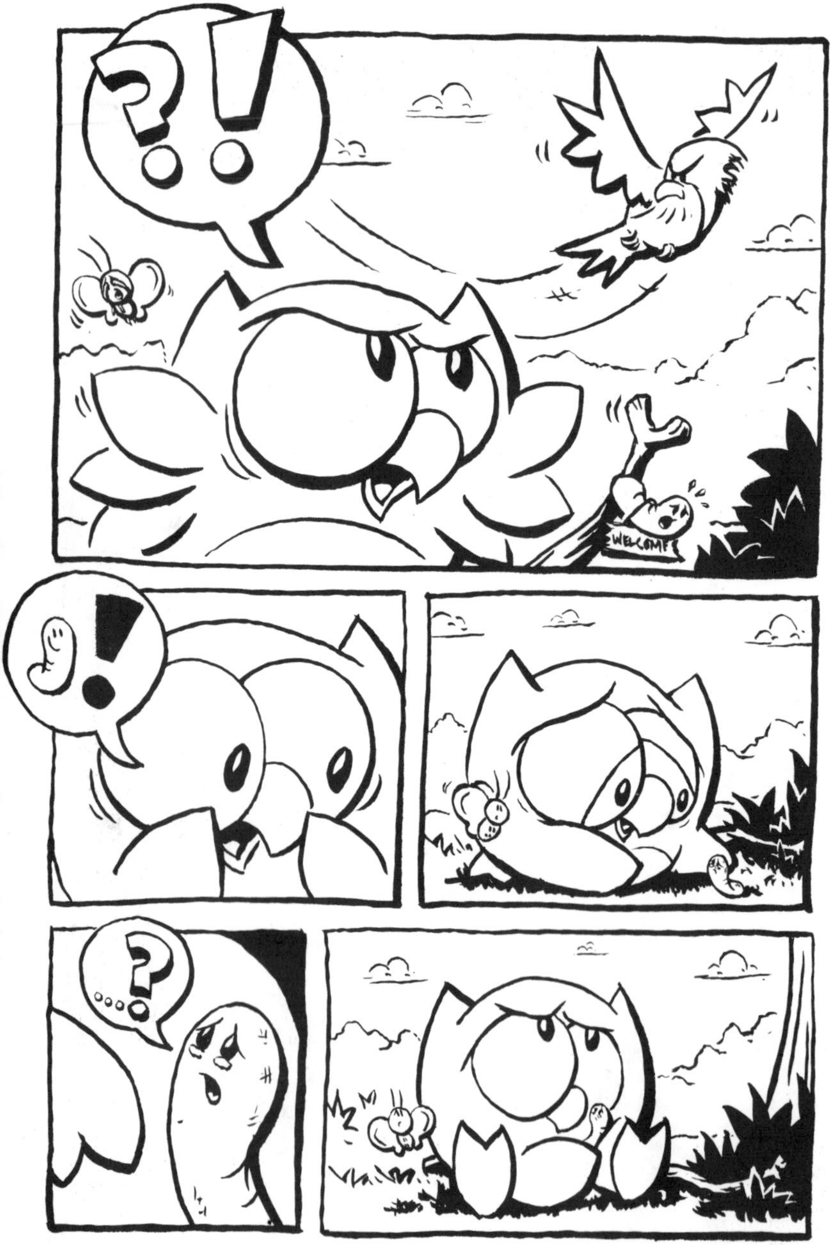
?!
WELCOME
!
?

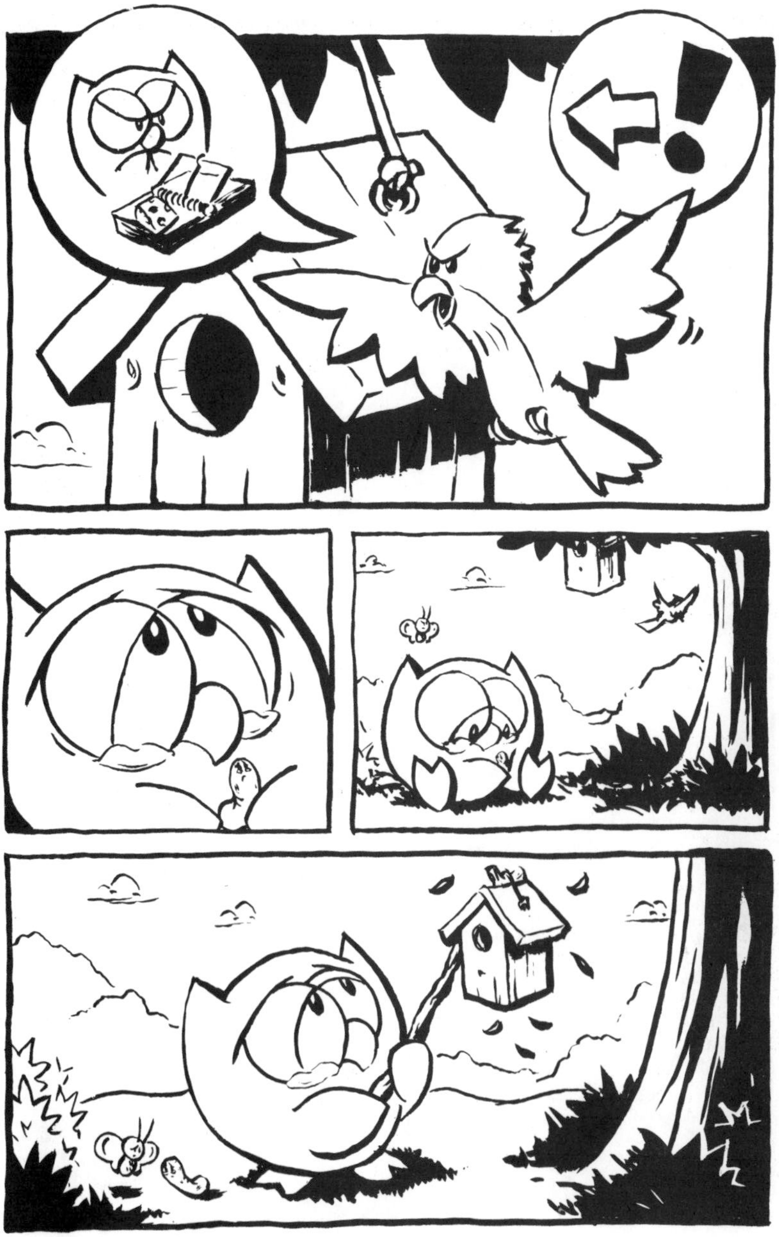
!

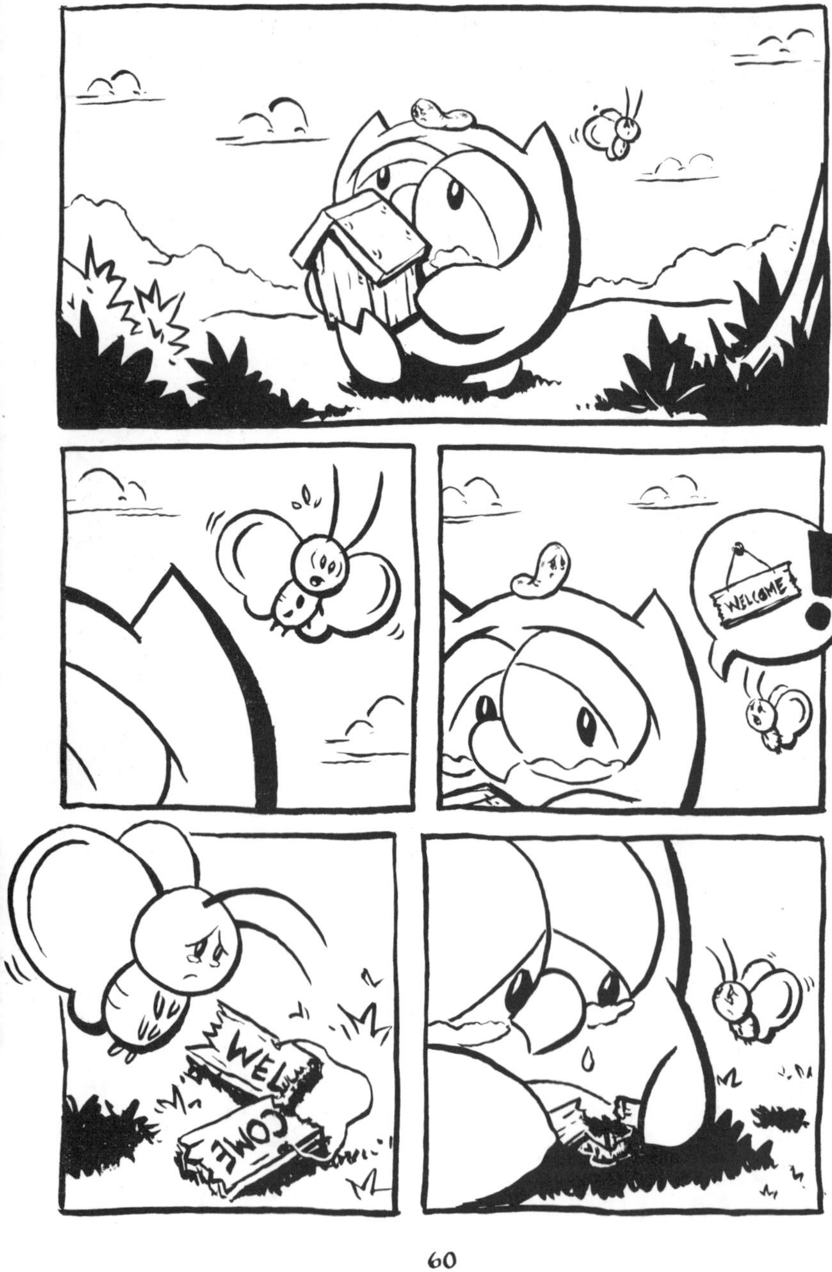
WELCOME
!
WEL
COME

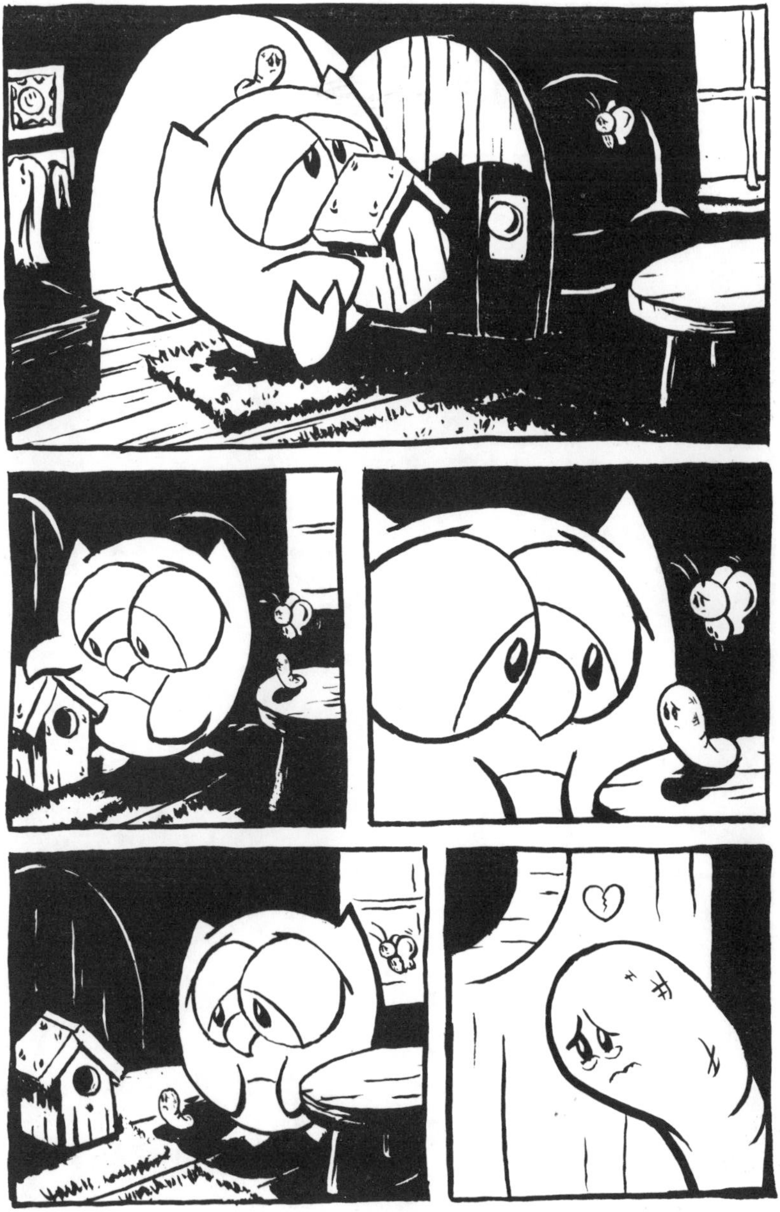

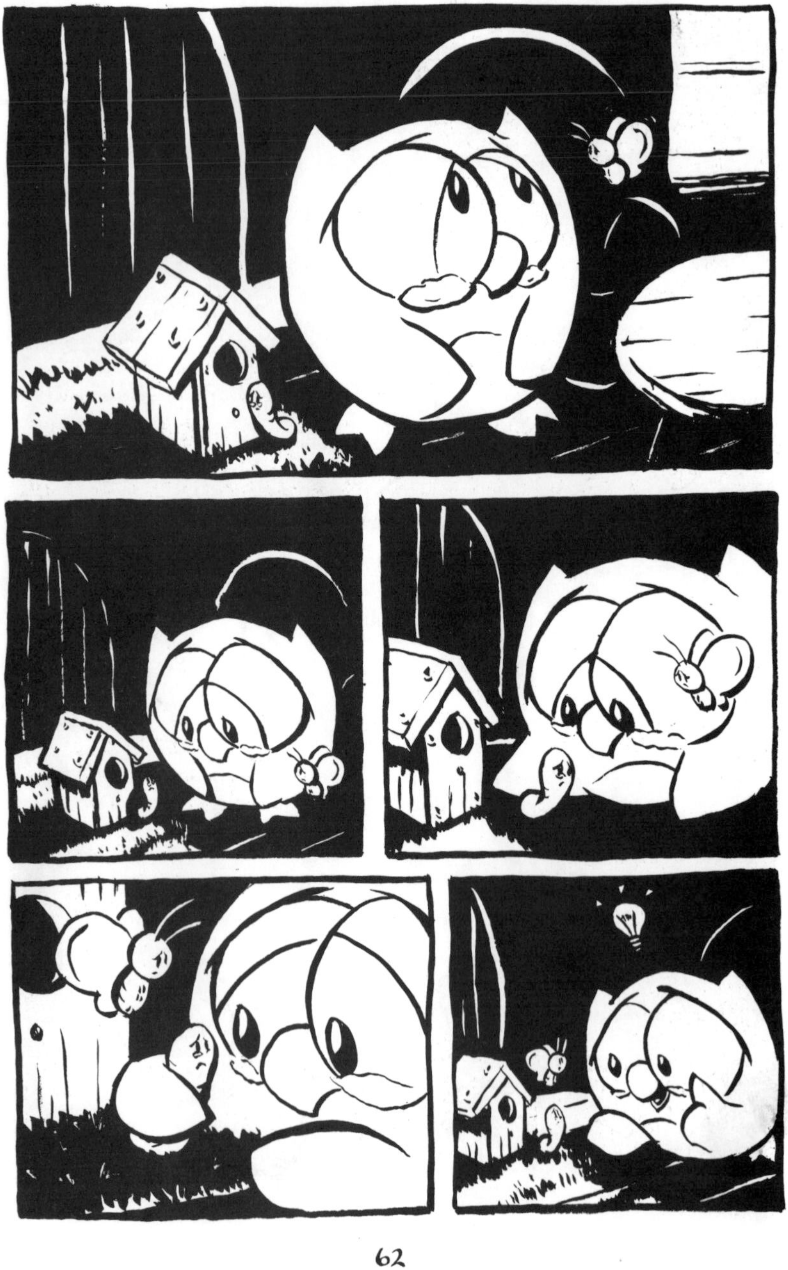

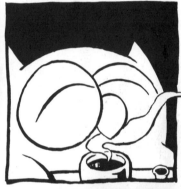

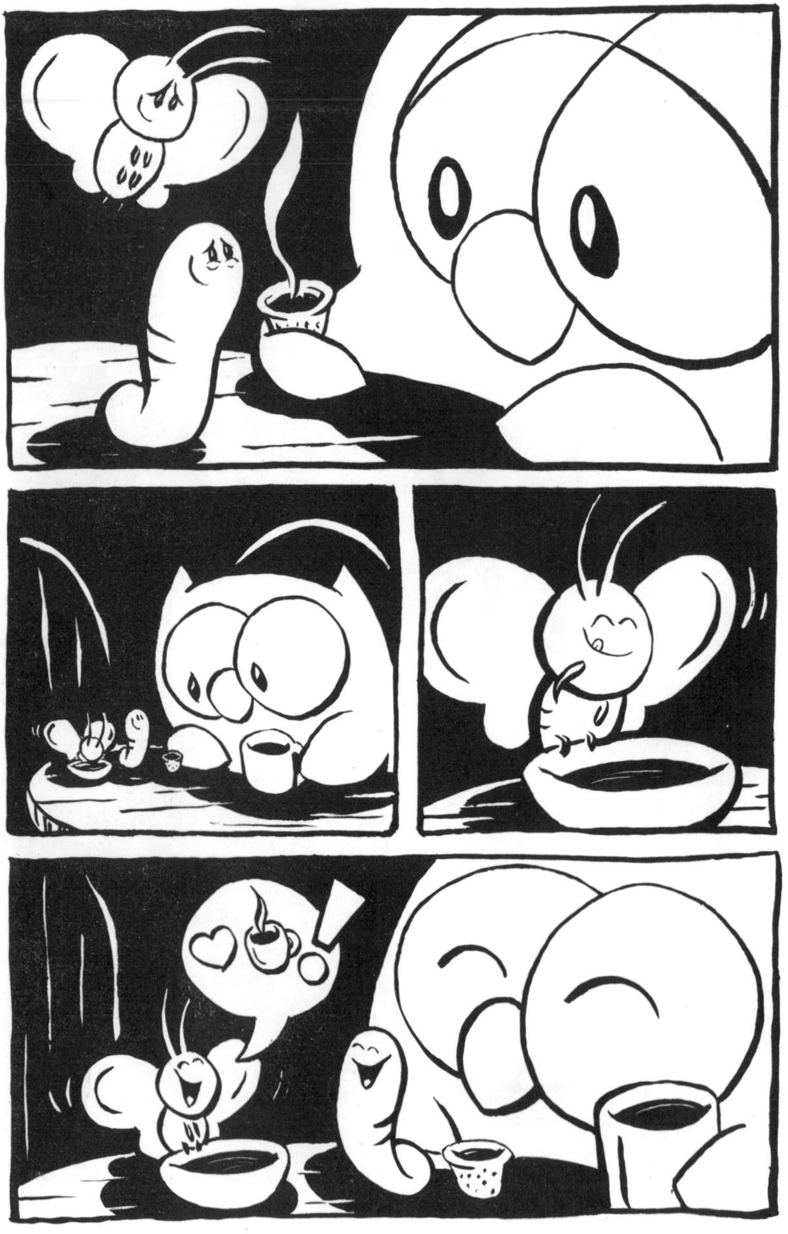

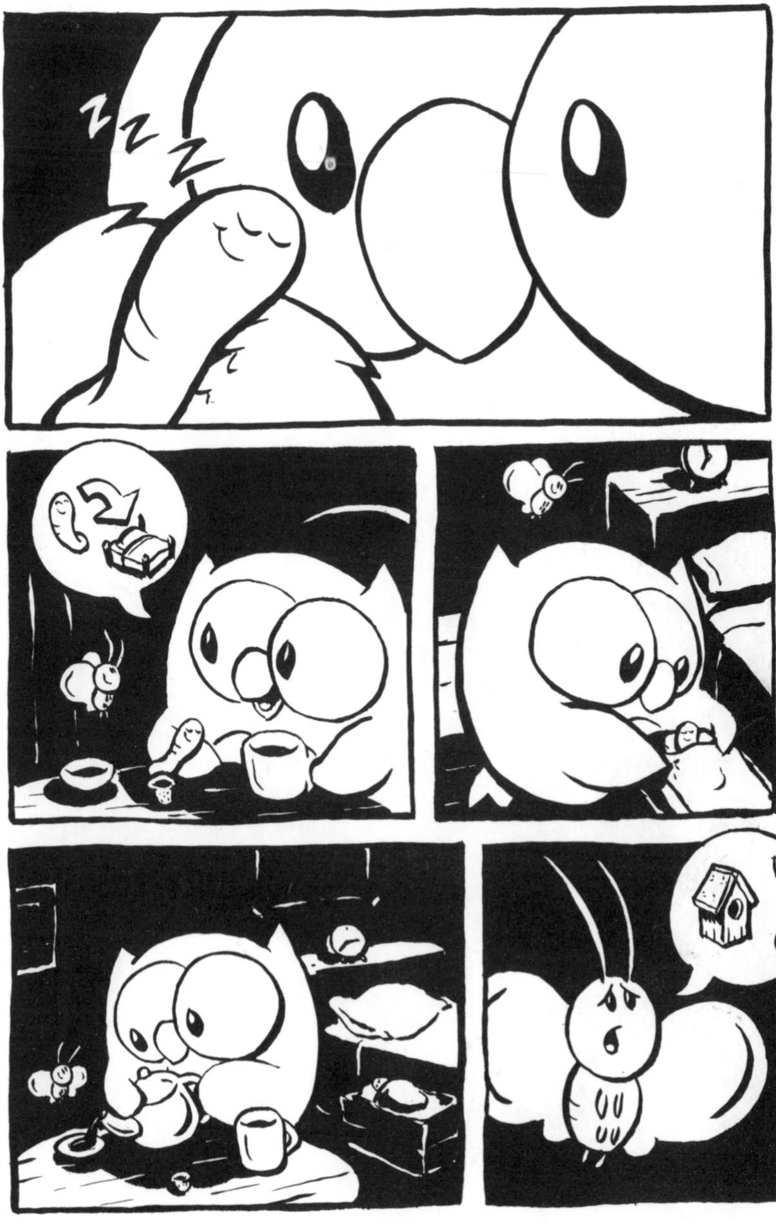
ZZZ
?

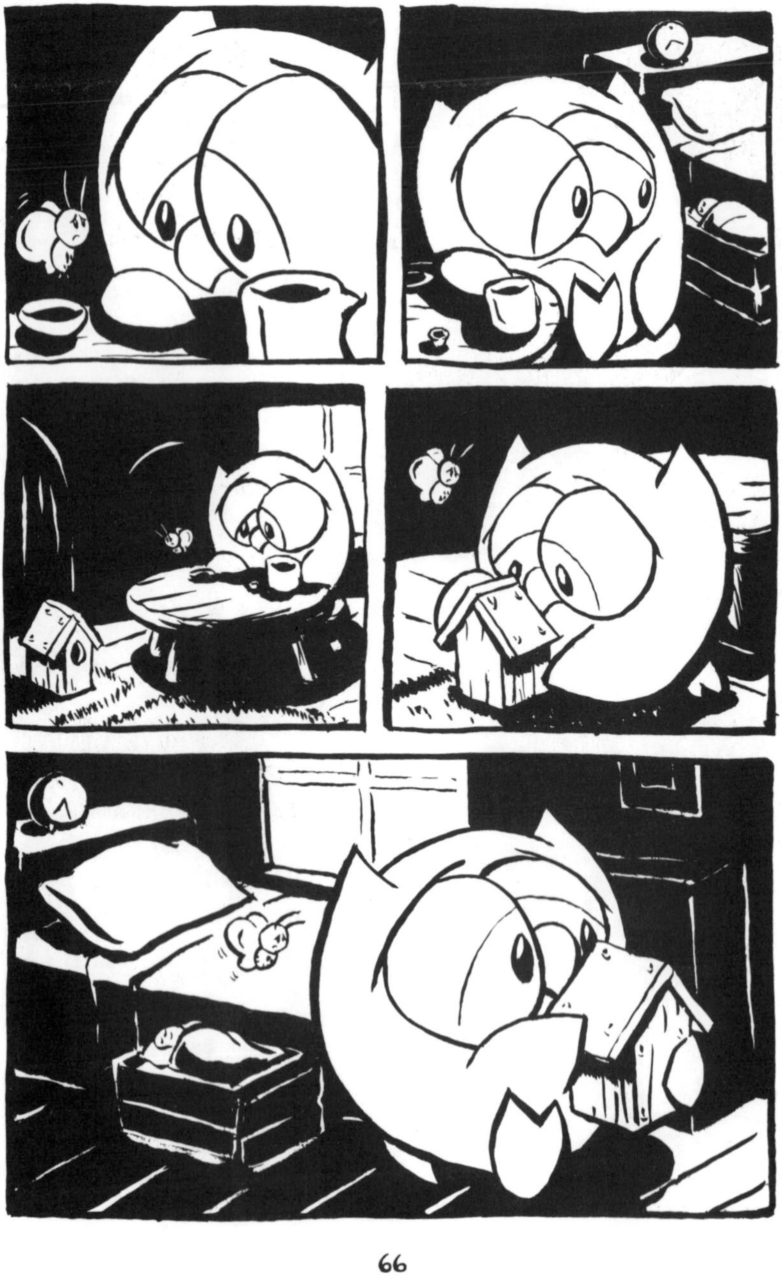

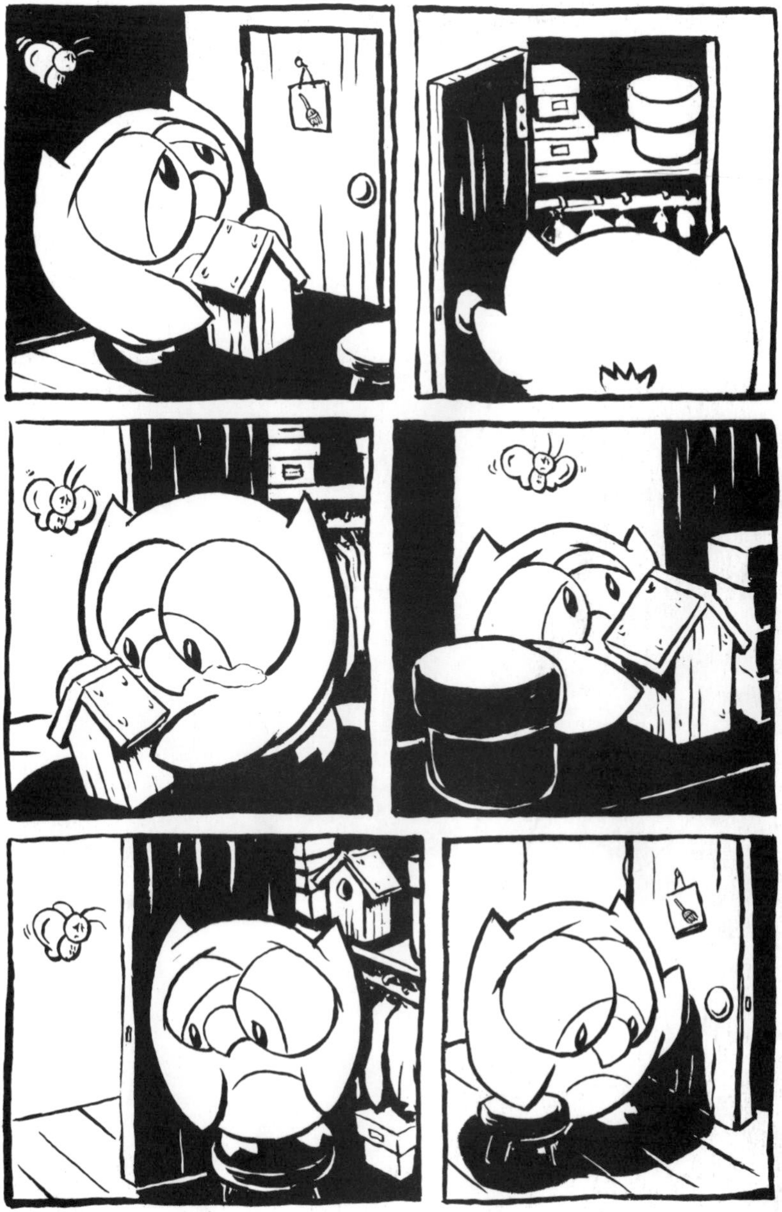

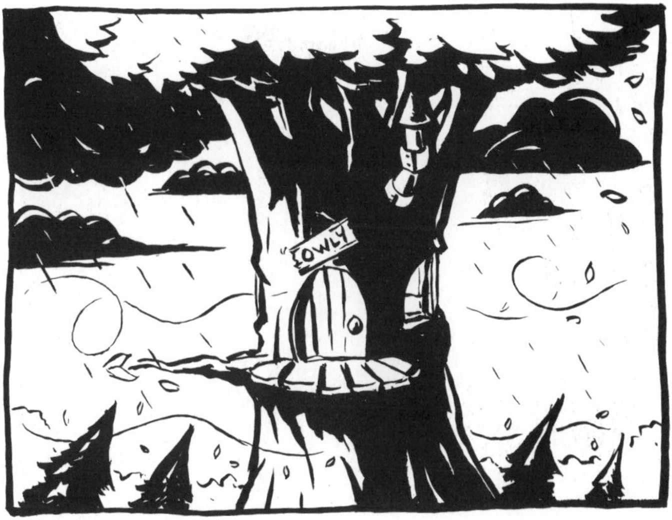
OWLY

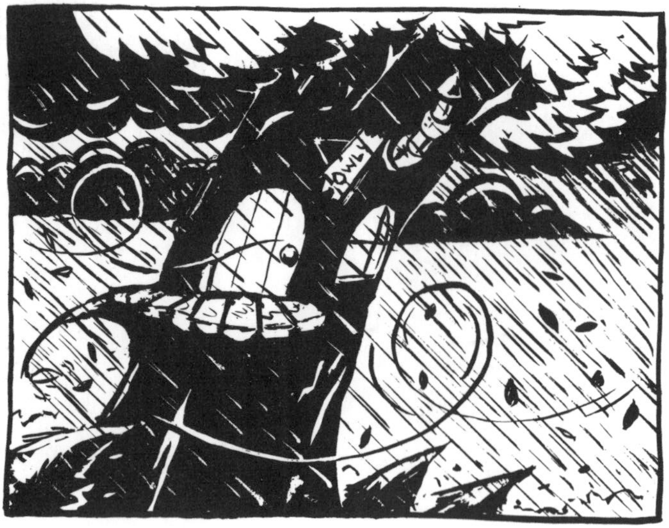
OWLY

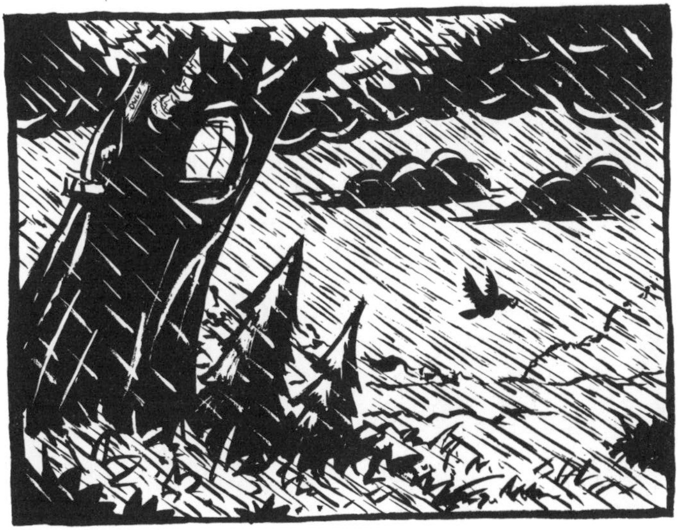
OWLY

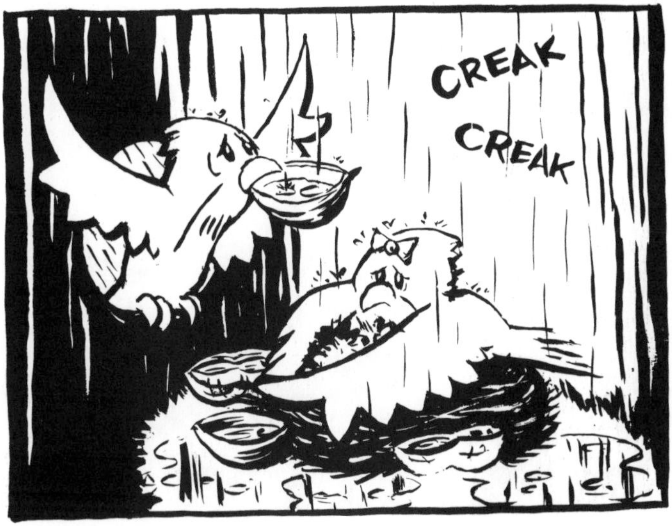
CREAK
CREAK

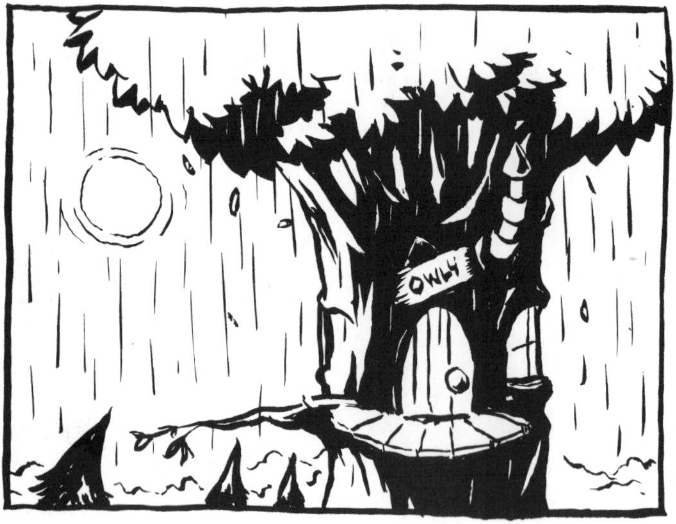
OWLY

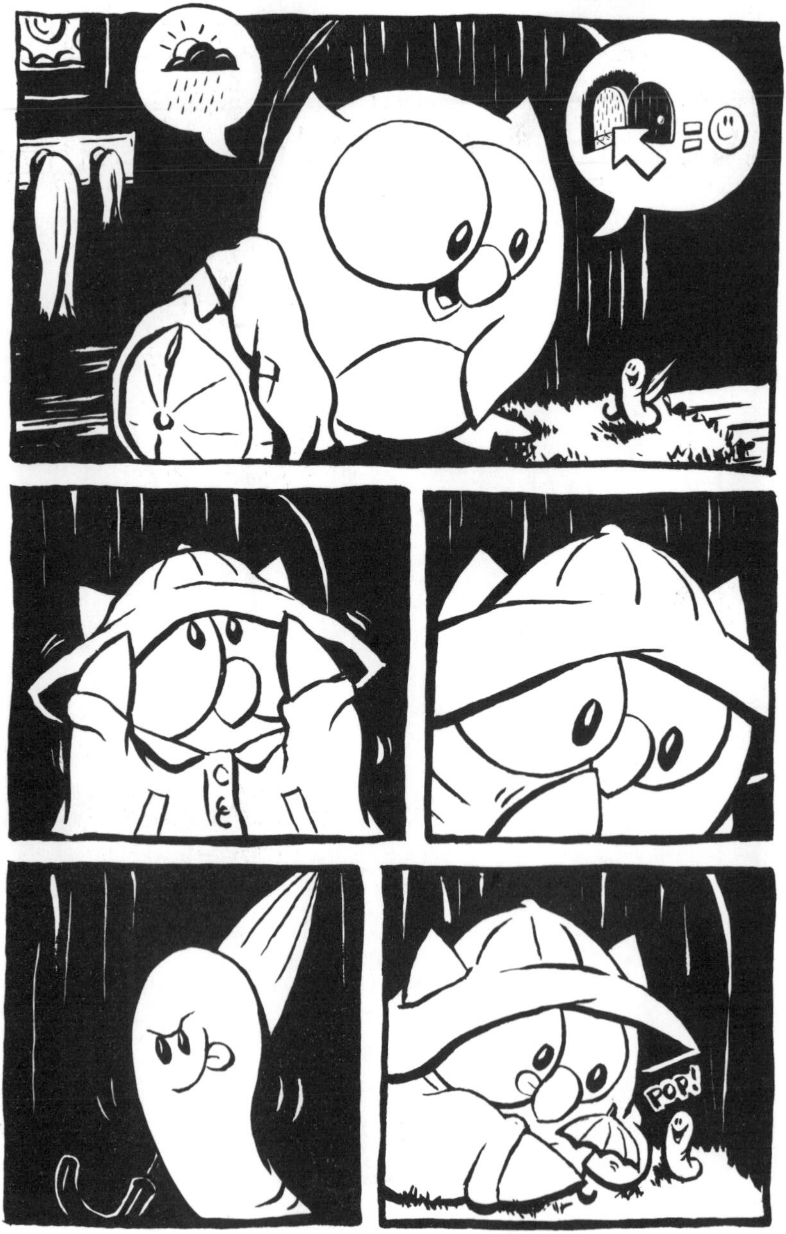
POP!

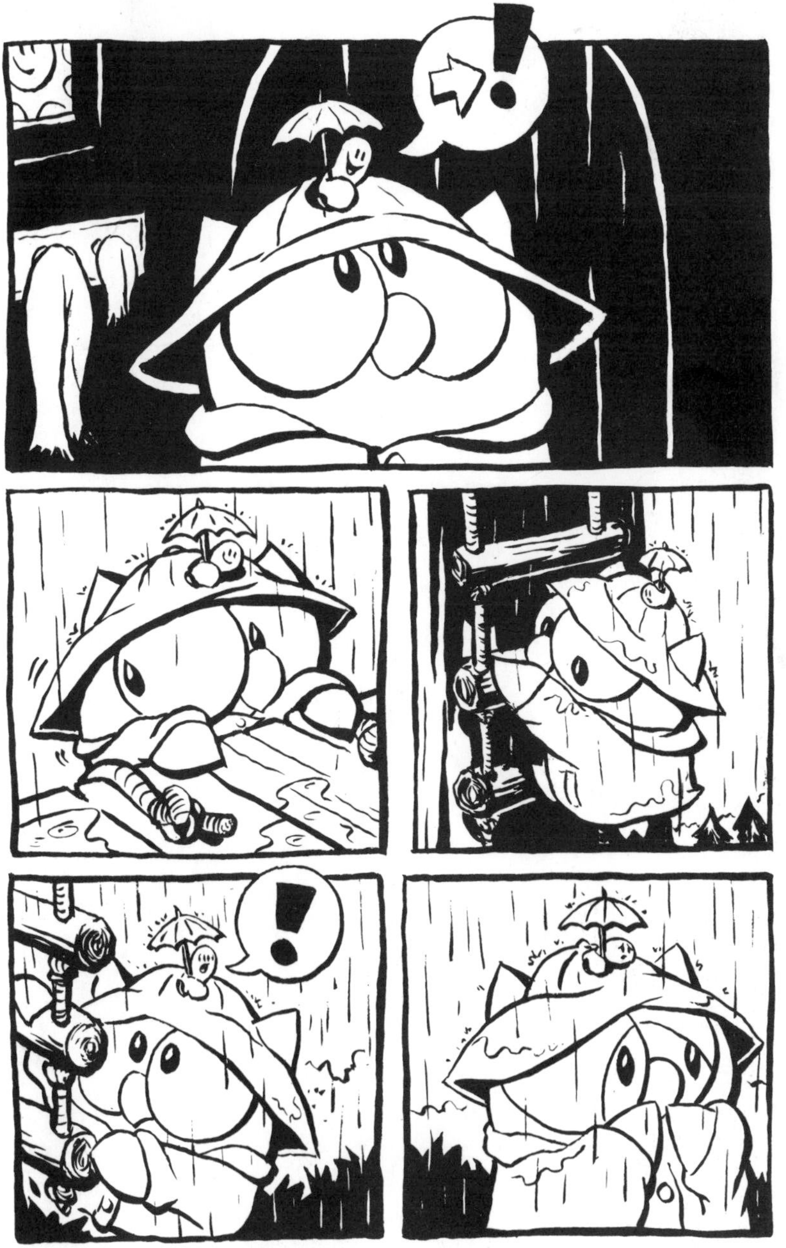
!
!

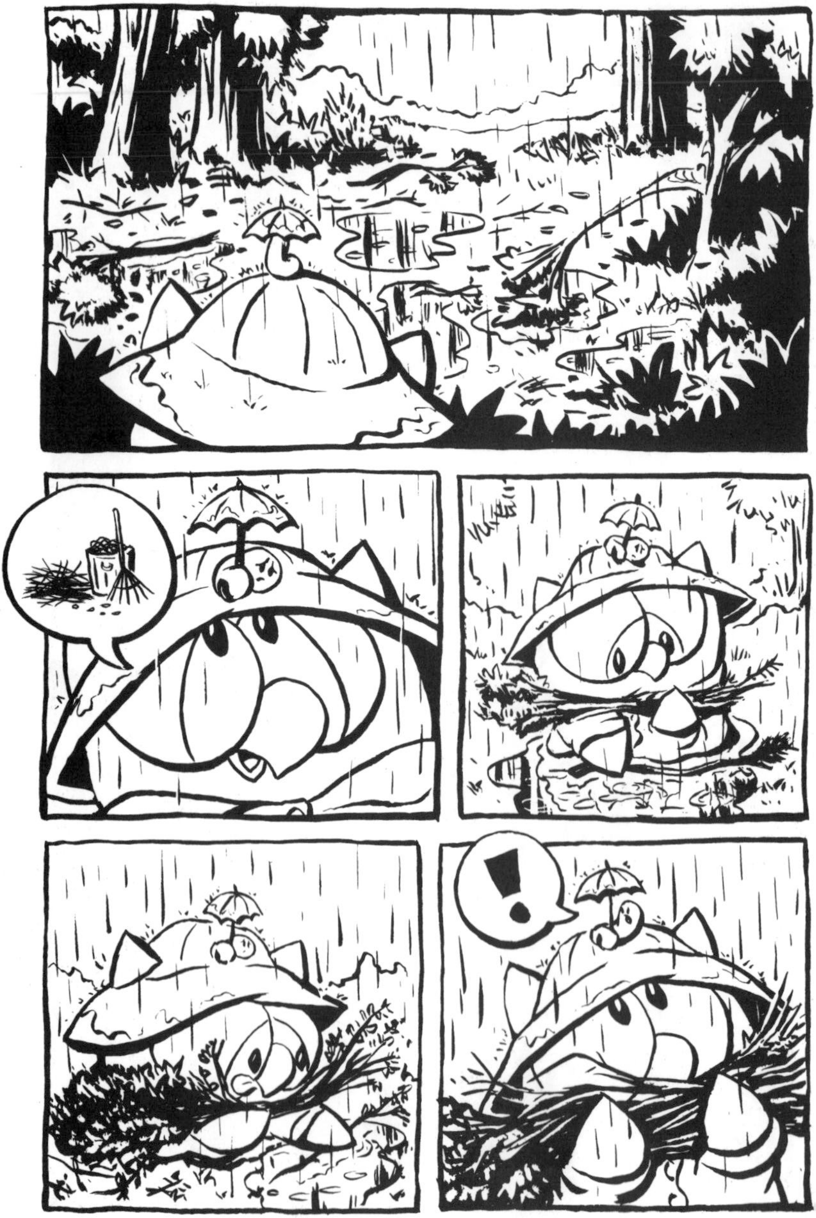
!

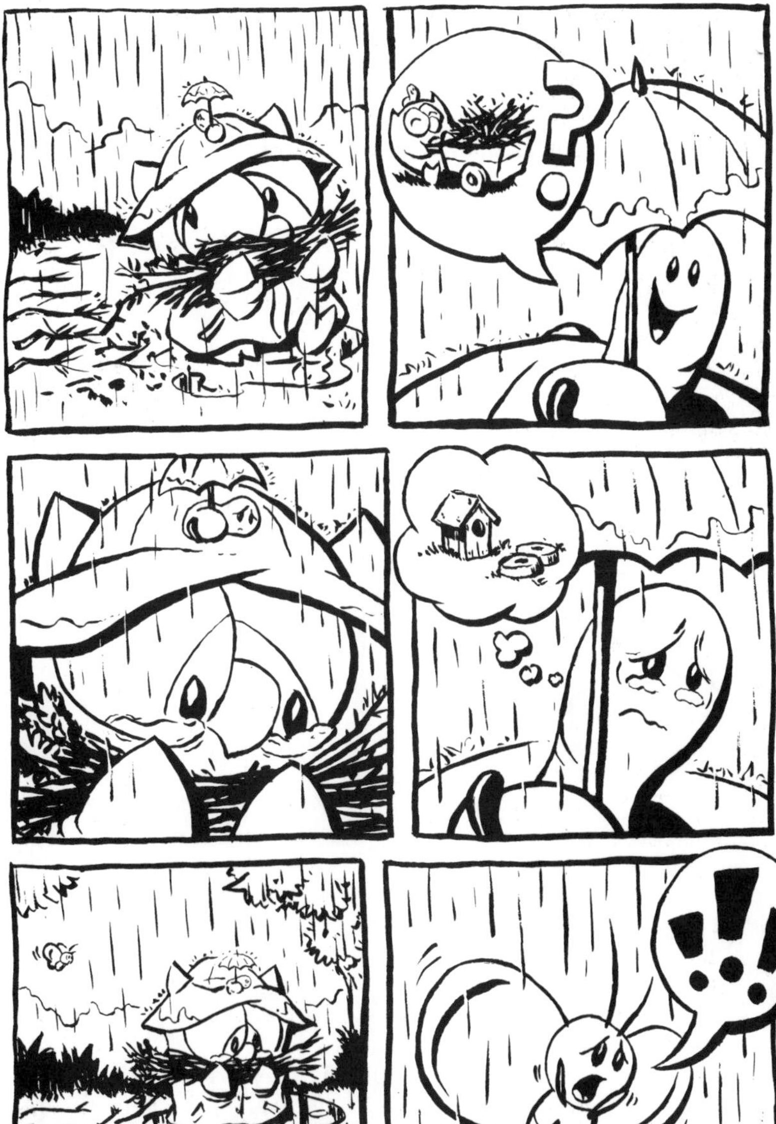
?
!

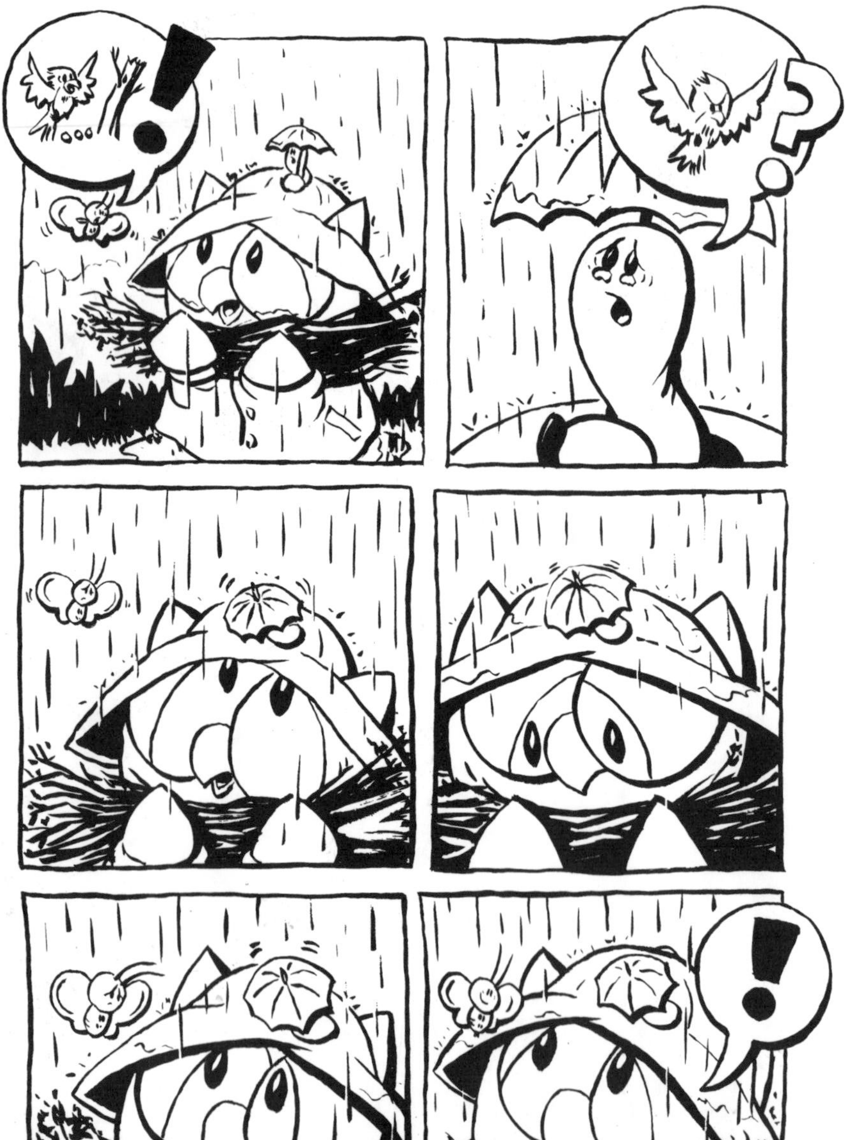

!
?
!

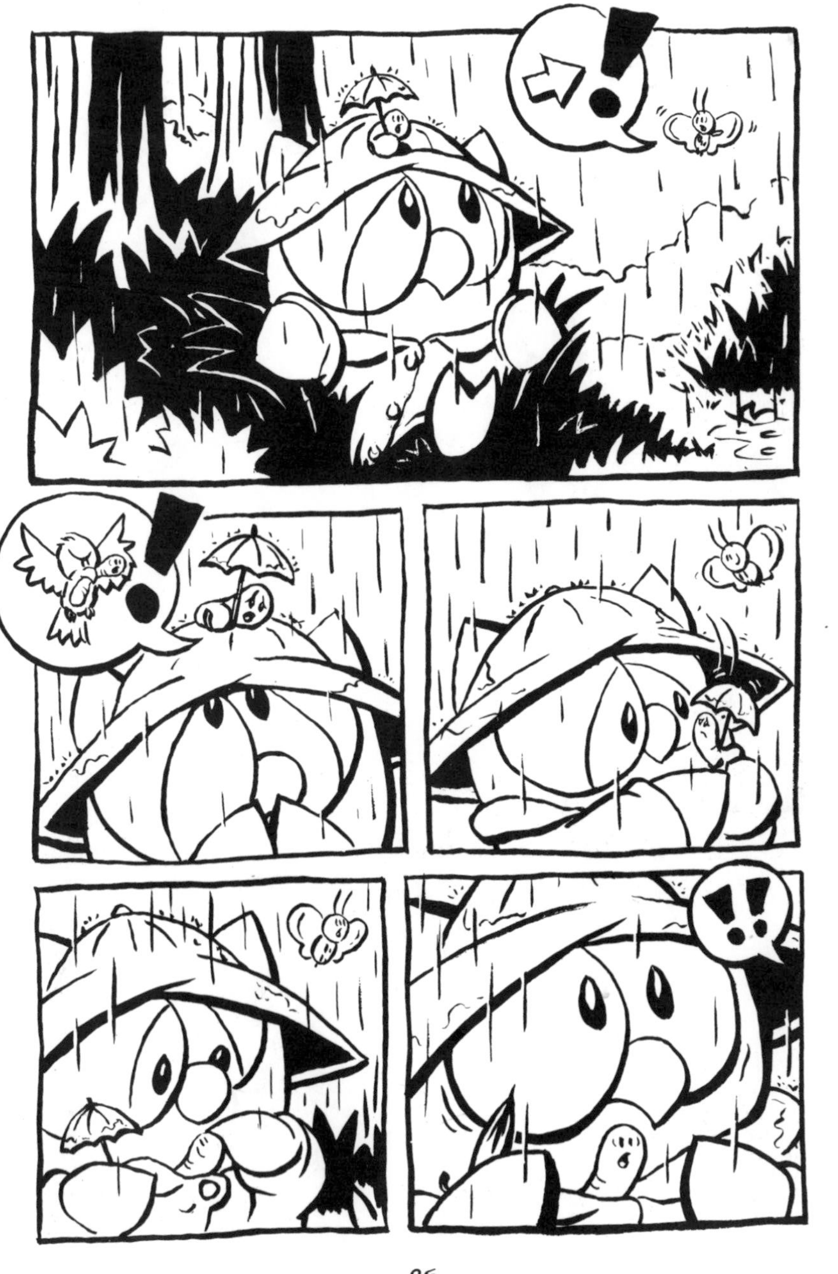

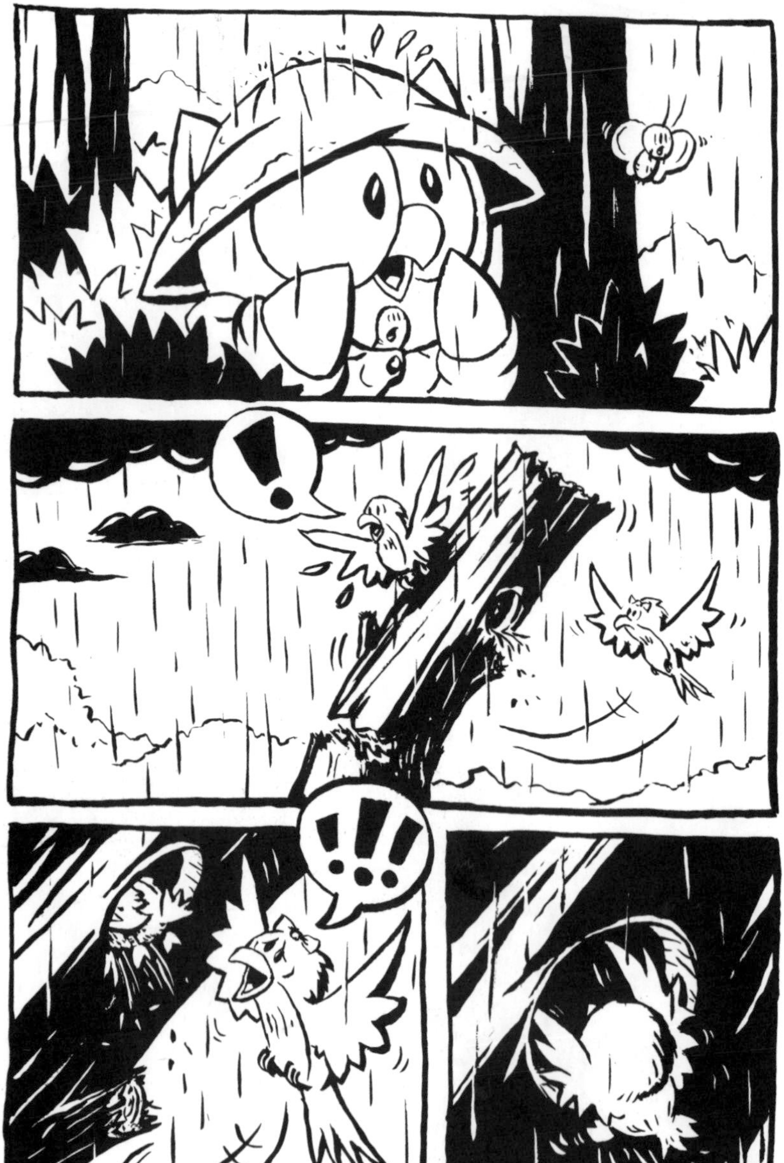
!
!!...!

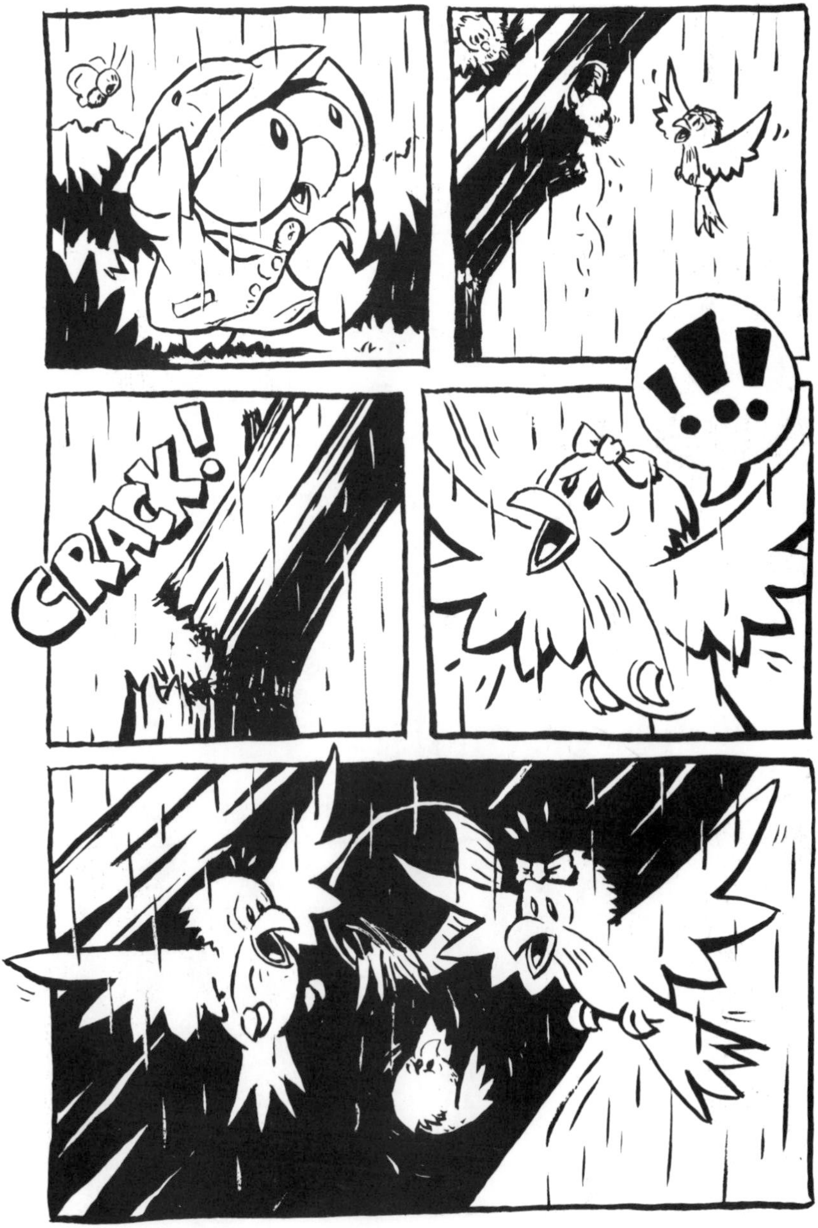
CRACK!
!!...

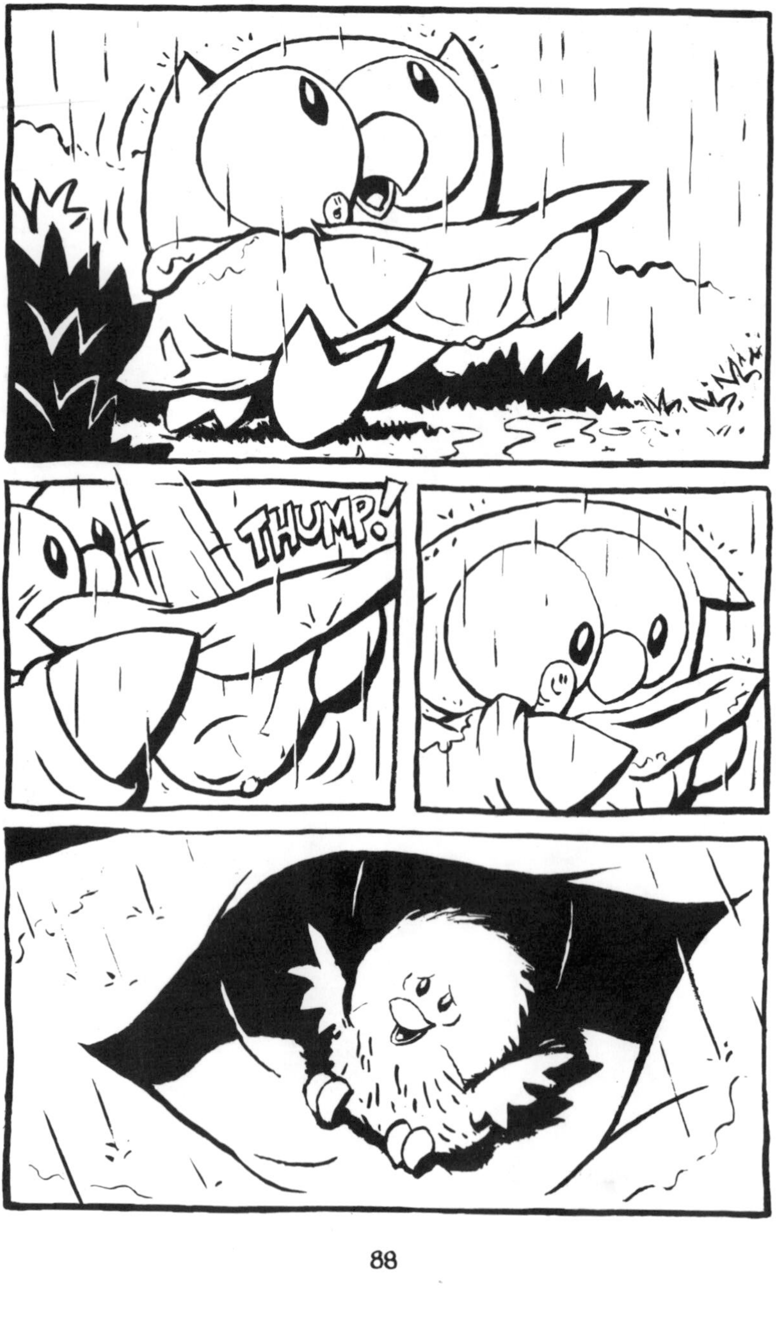
THUMP!

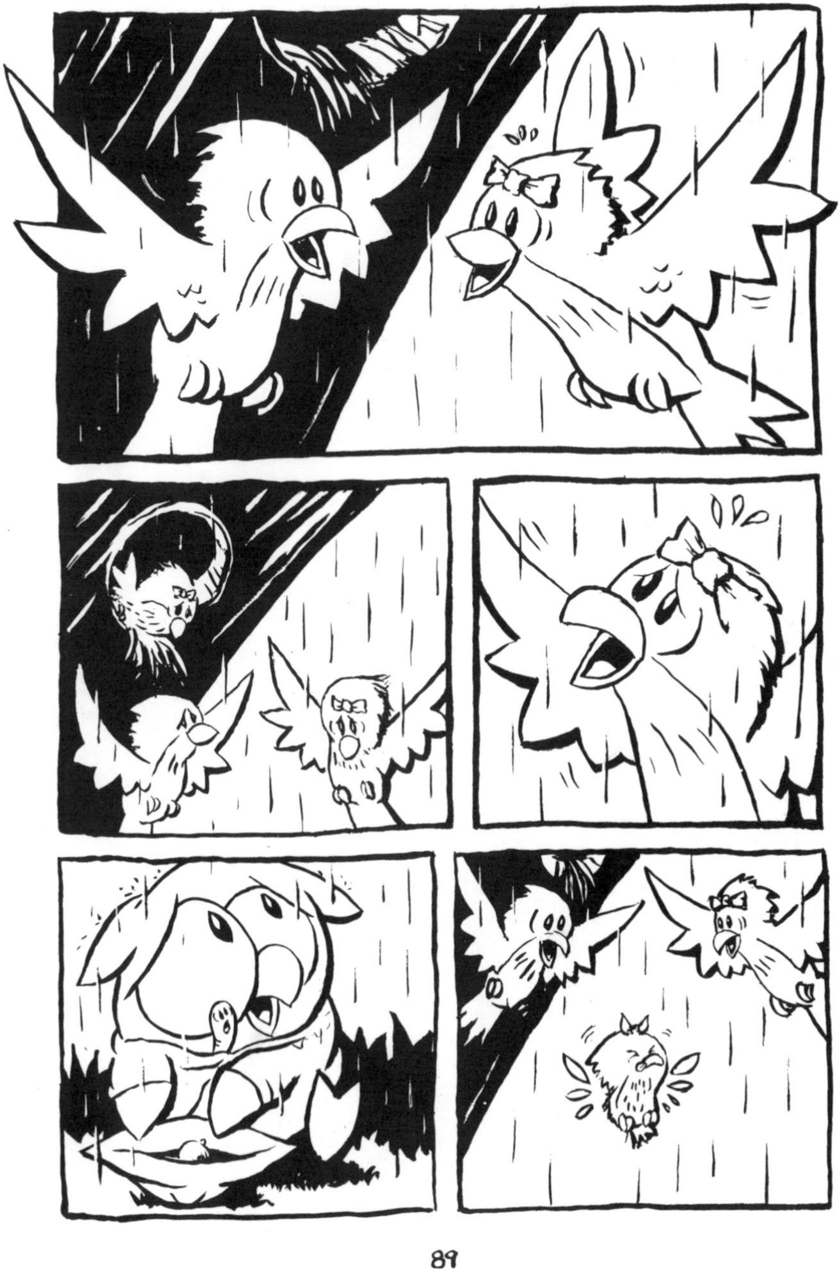

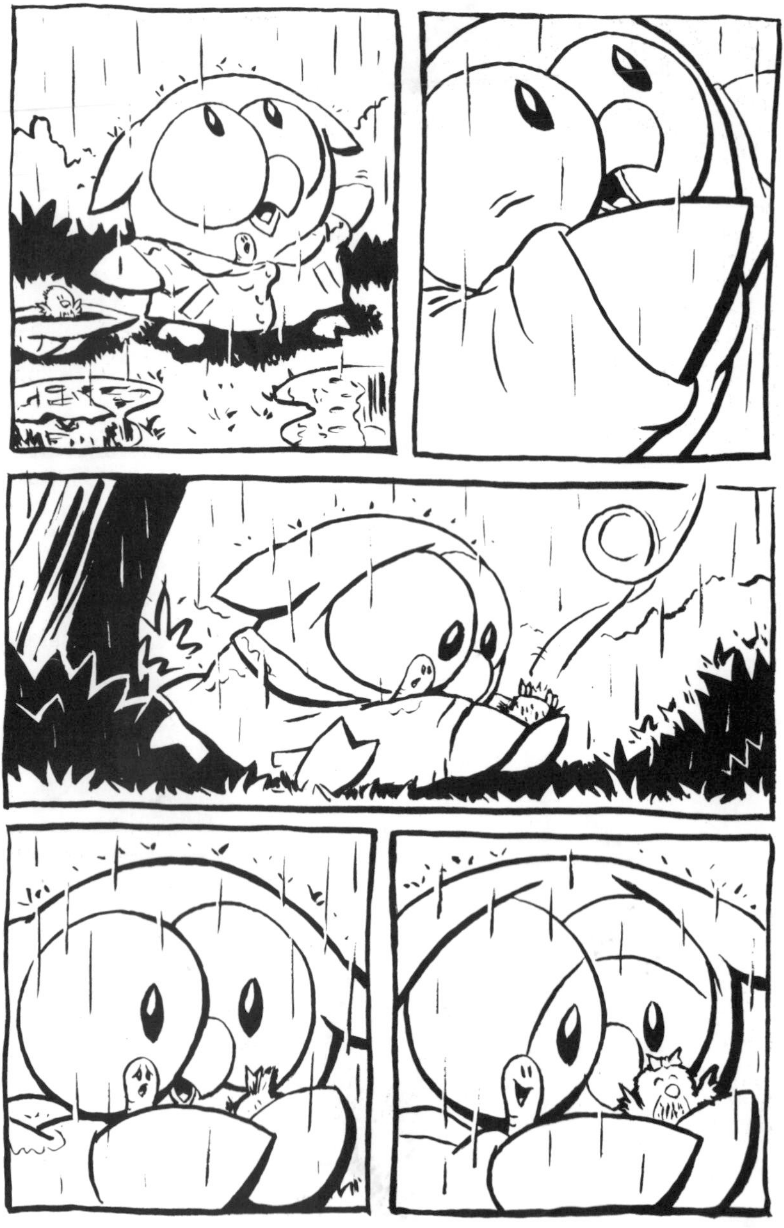

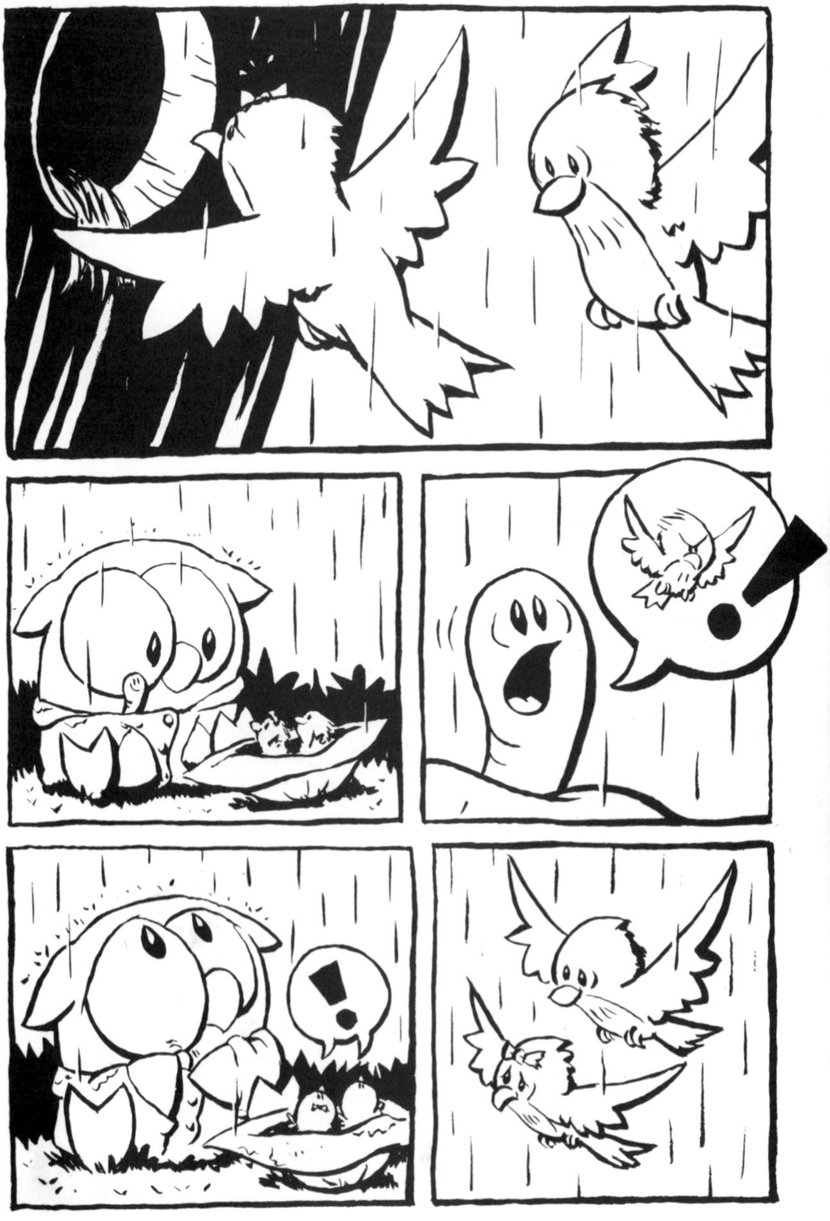
!
!

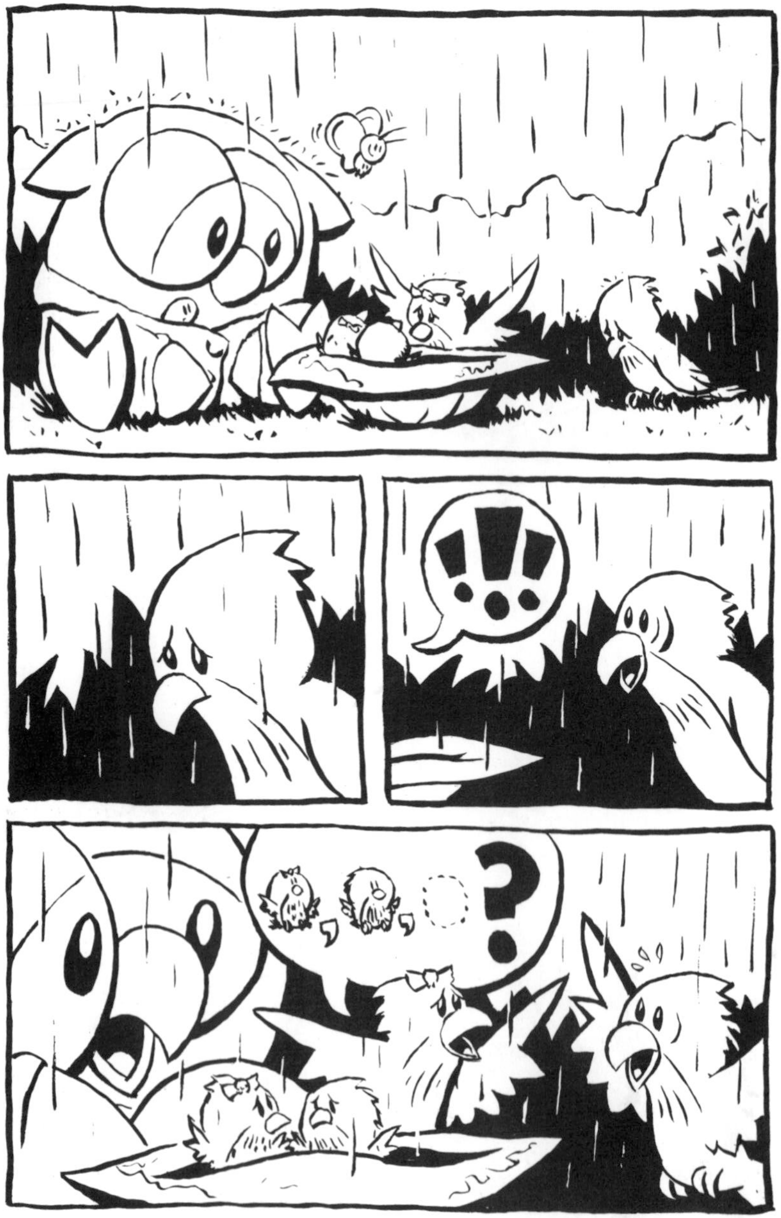
!!!
?

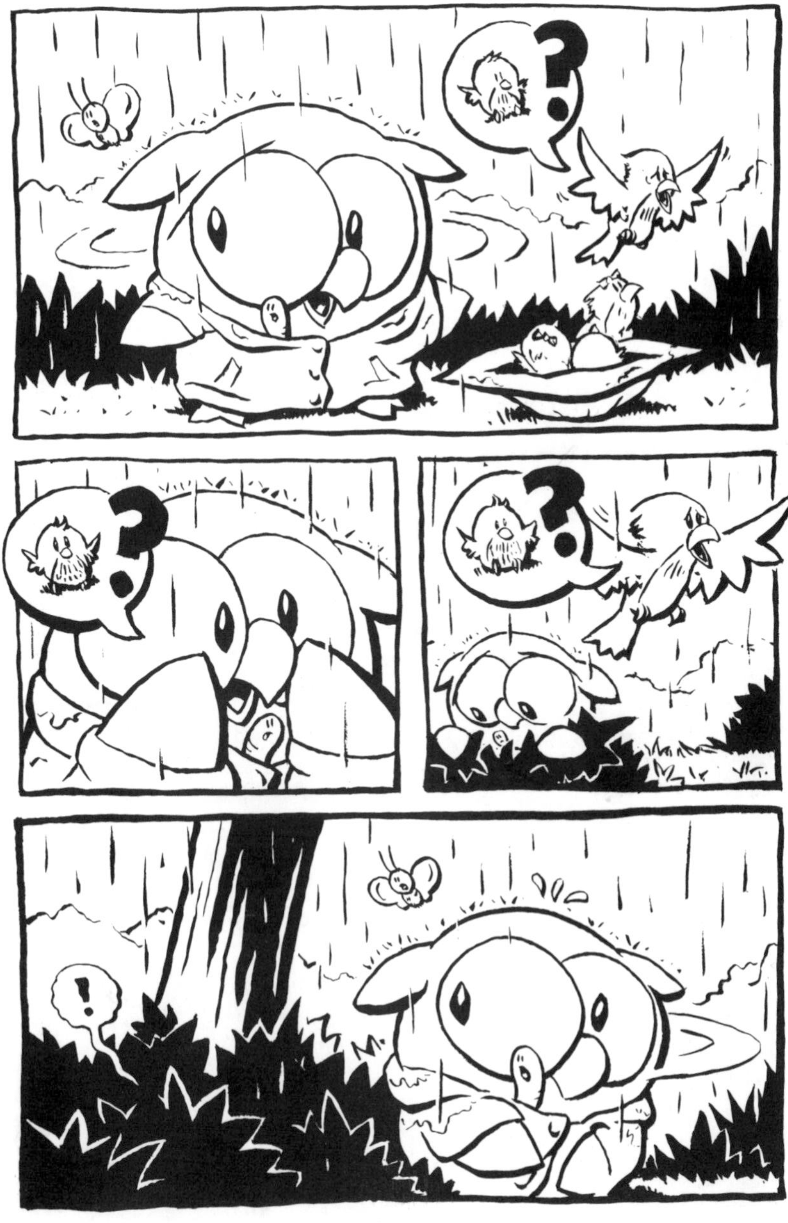
?
?
?
!

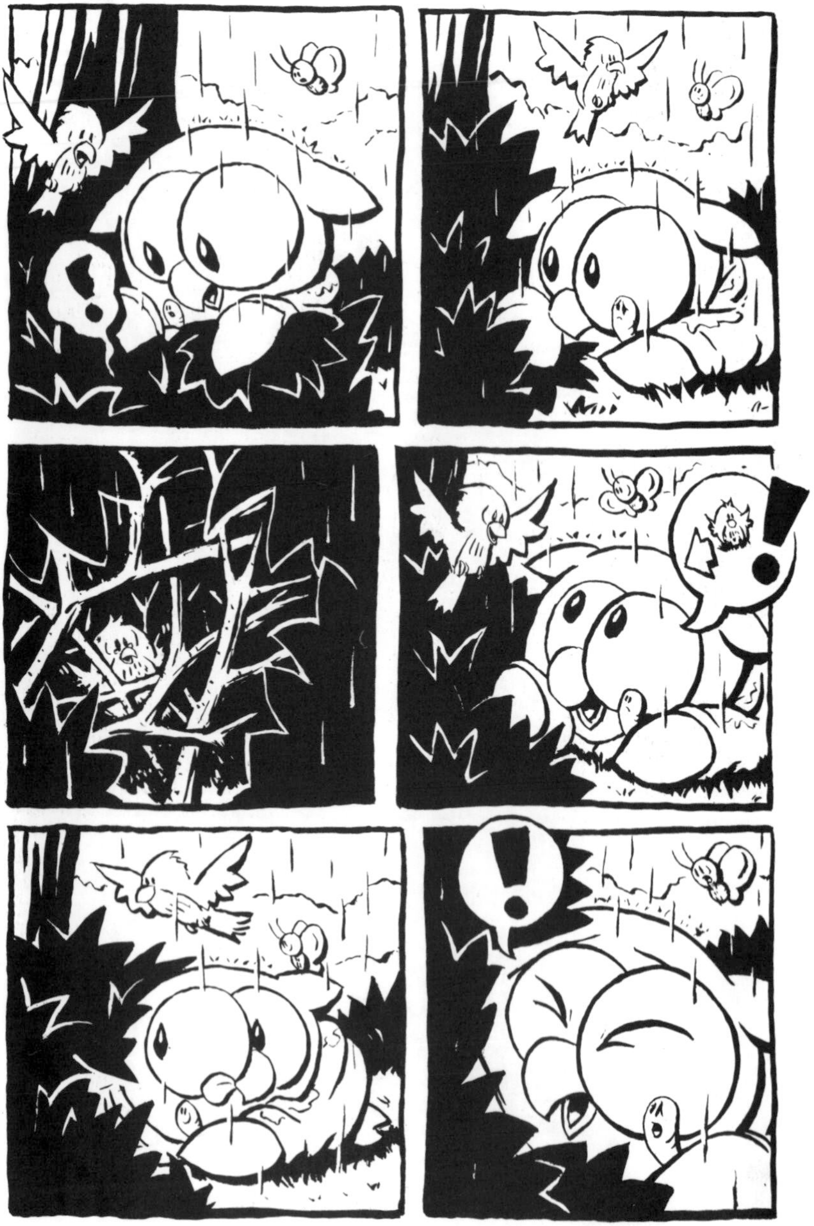
!
!
!

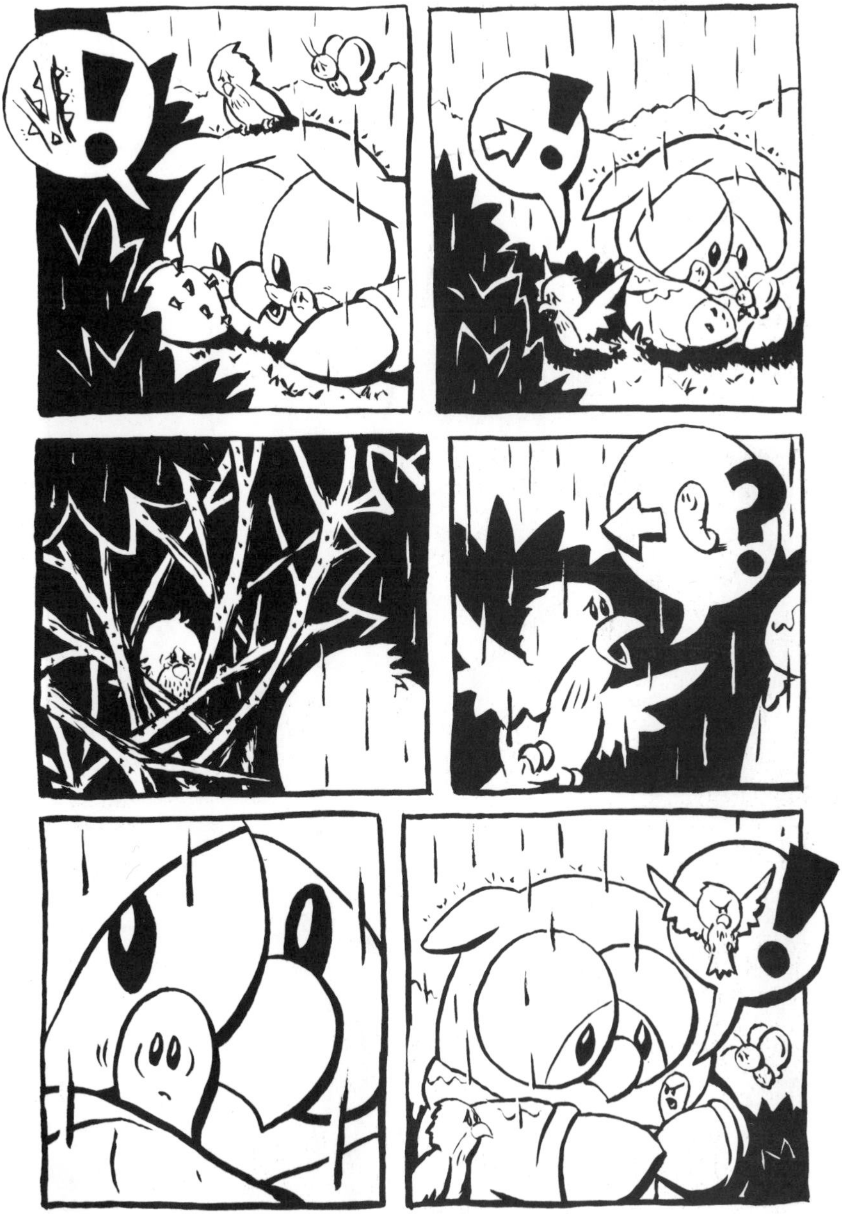
!
!
?
!

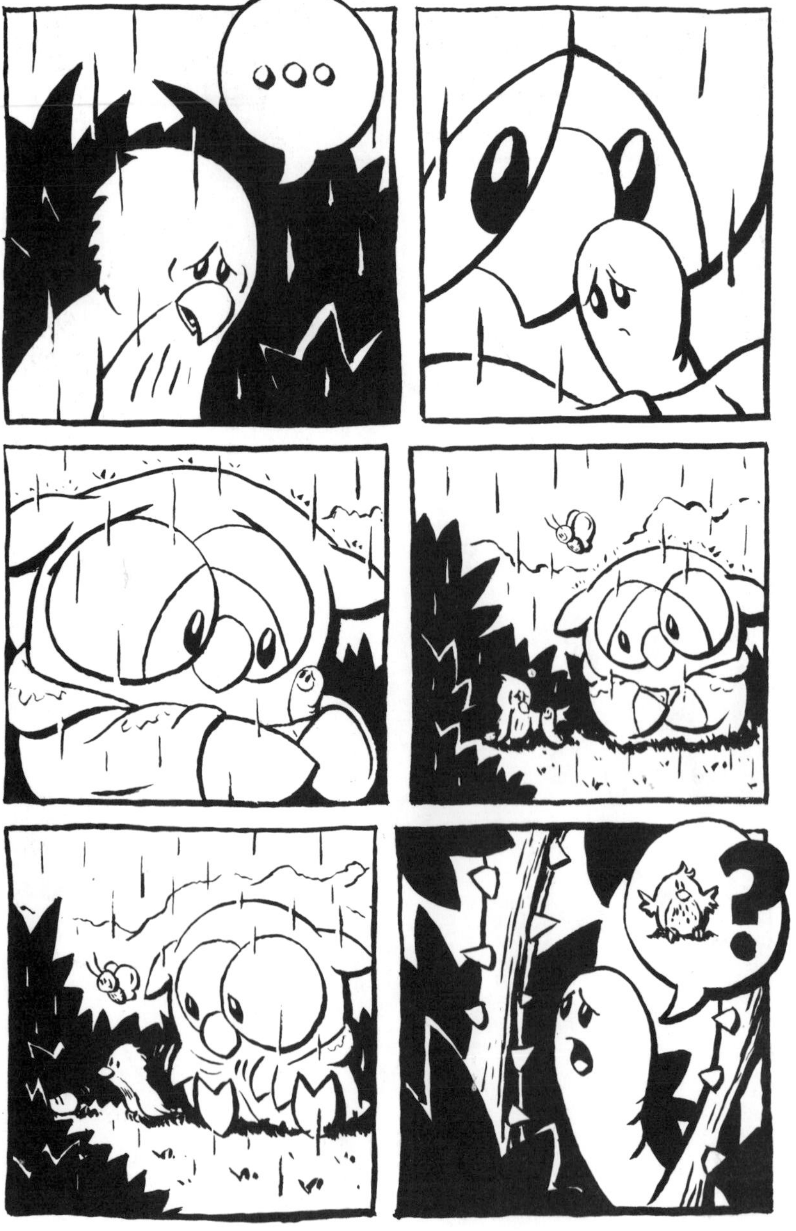
...
?

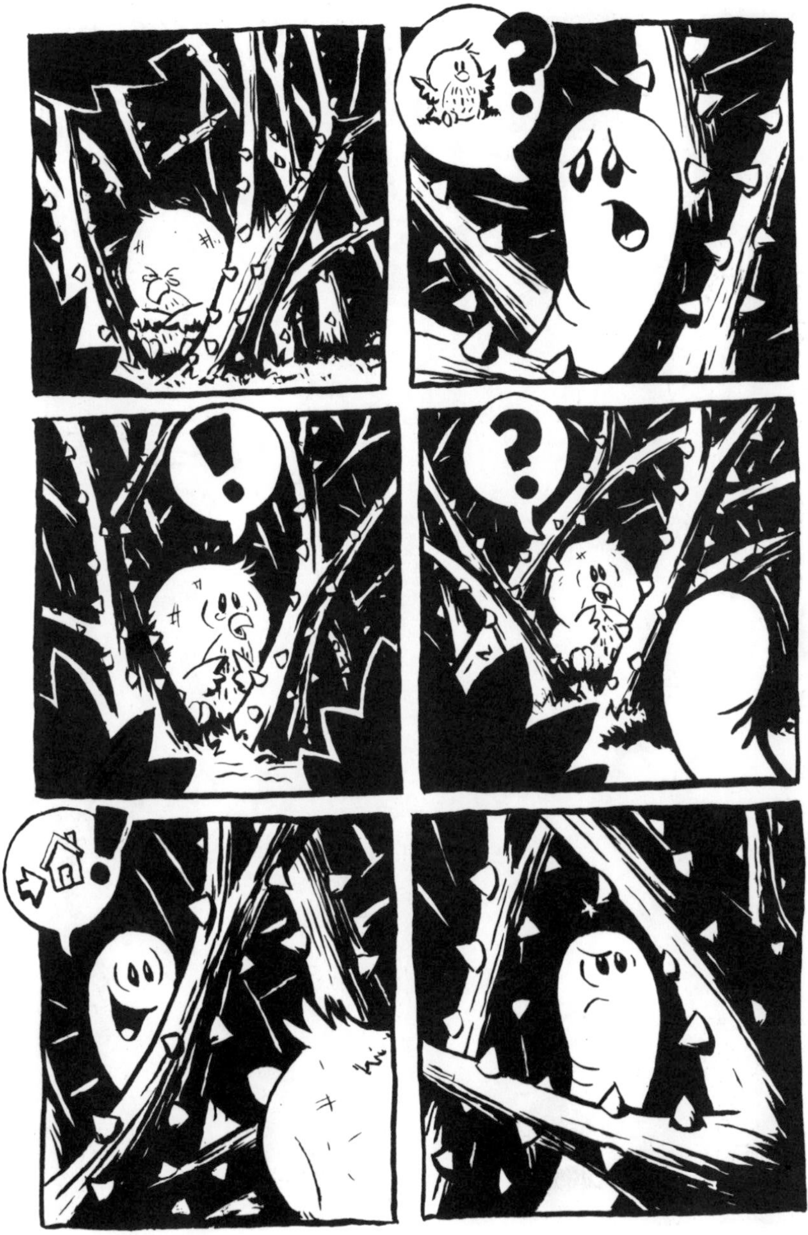

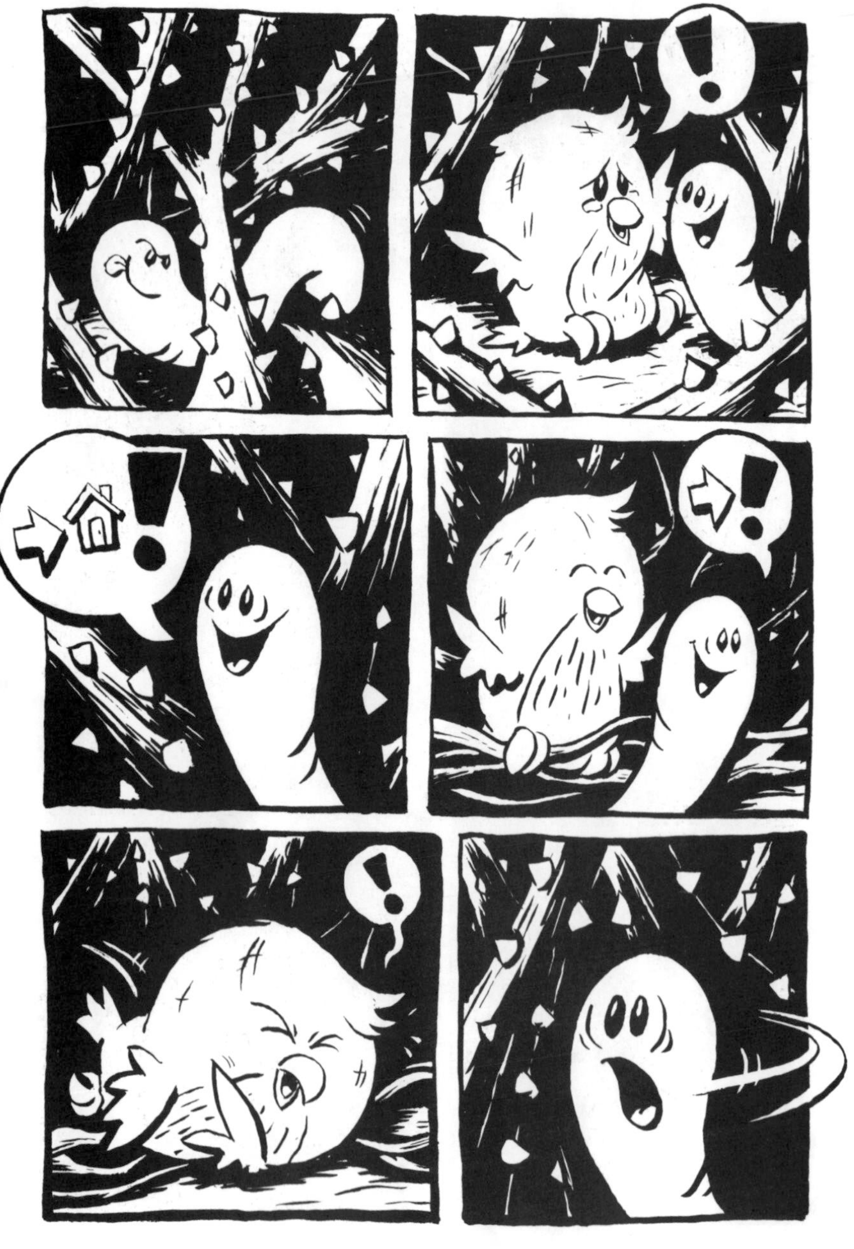

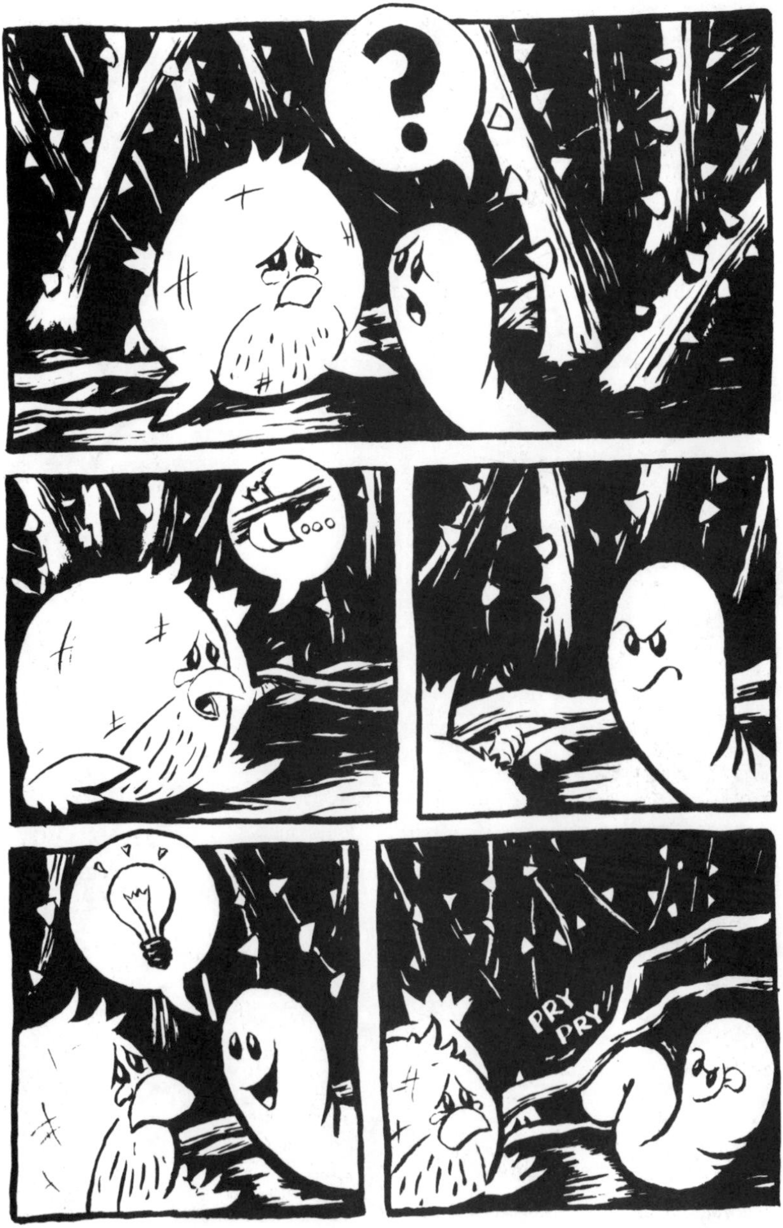
?
PRY
PRY

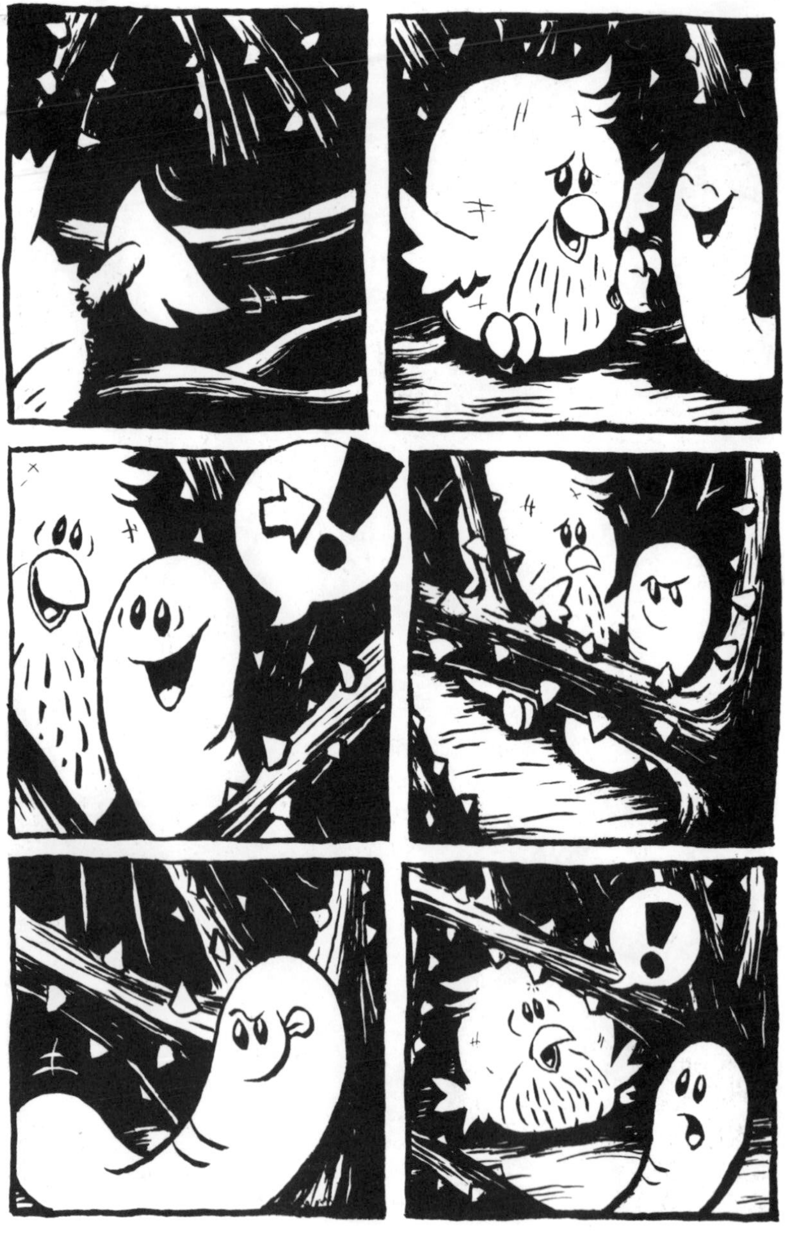
!
!

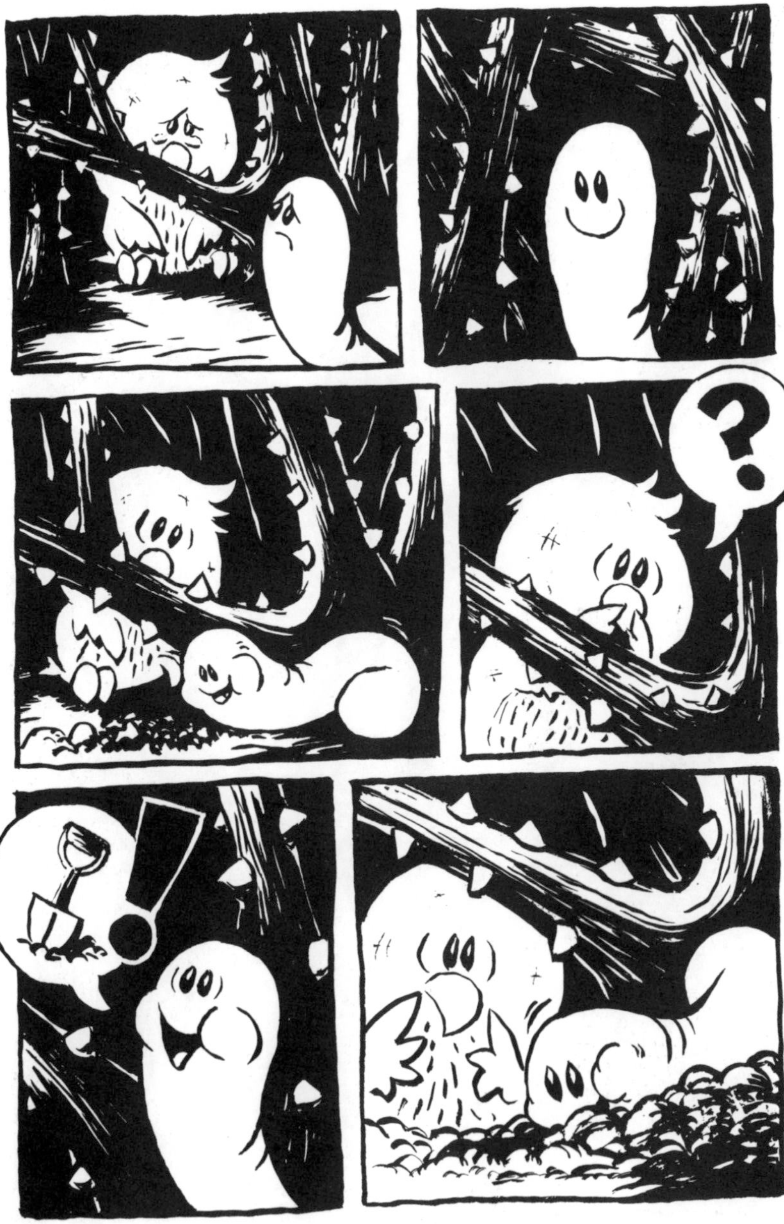
?
!

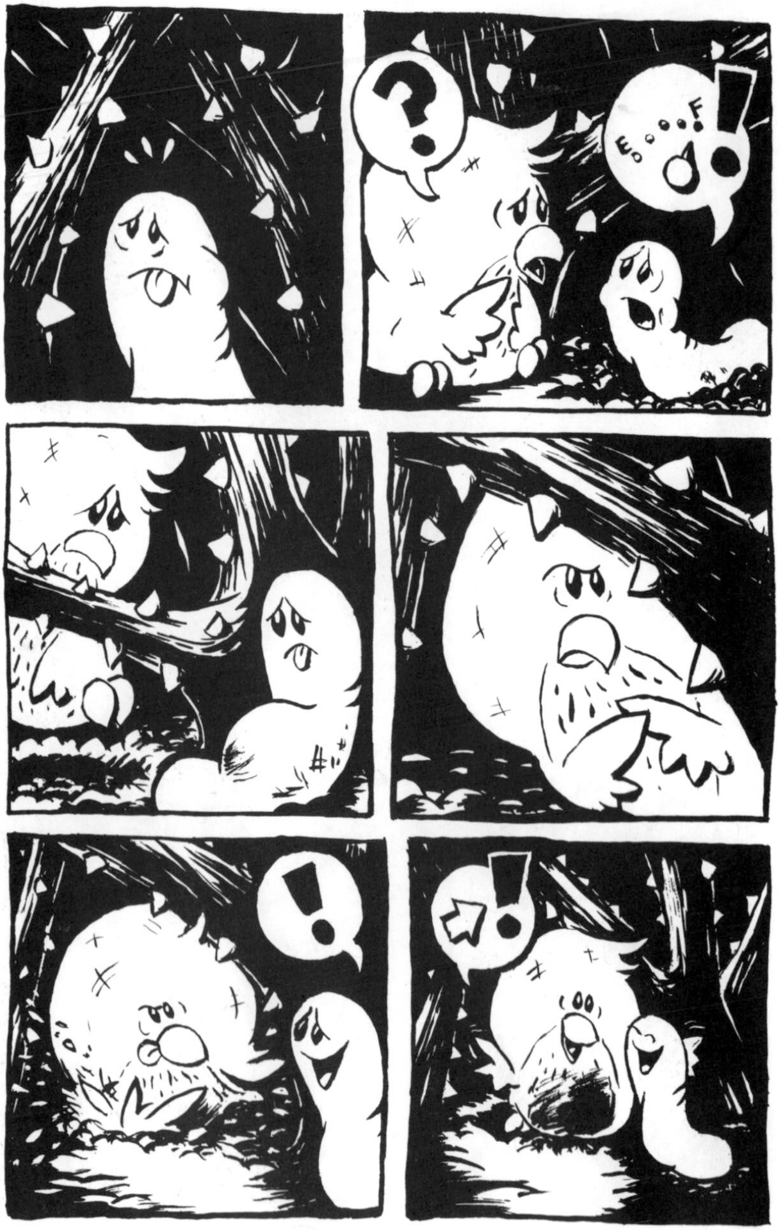
?
E...F!
!
!

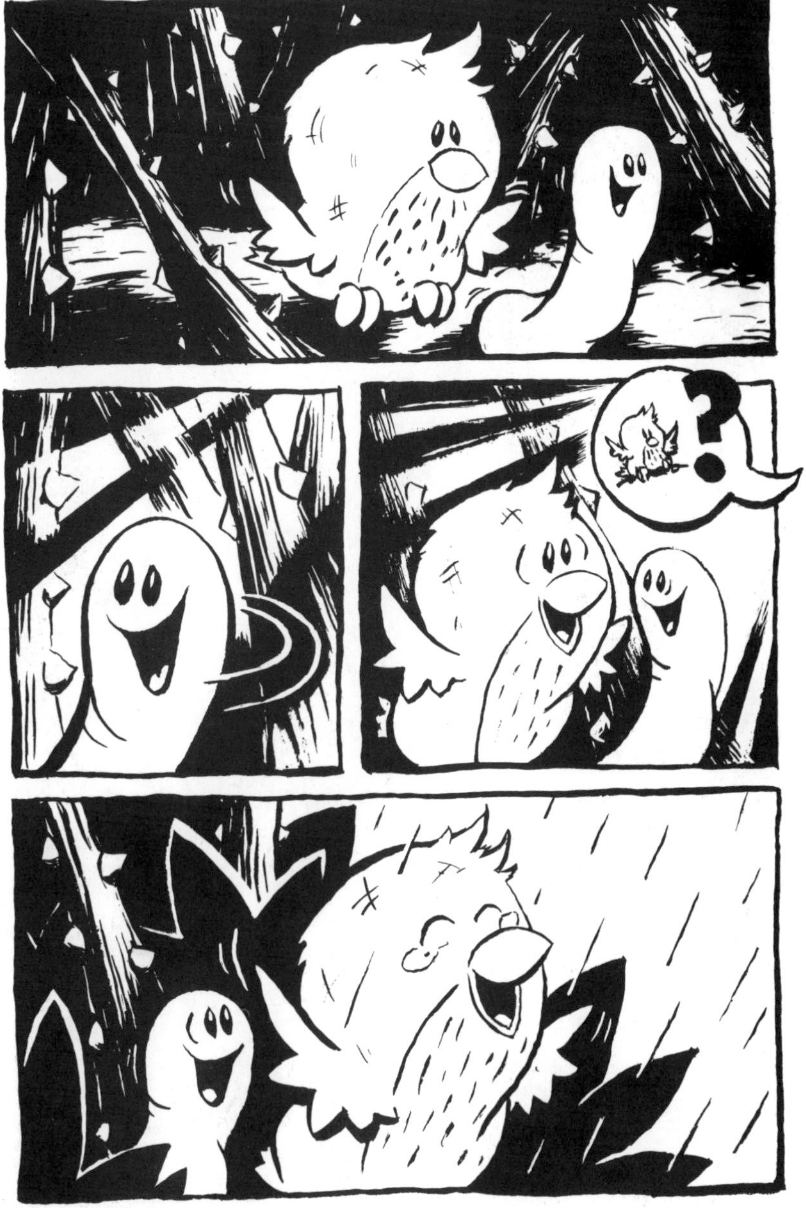
?

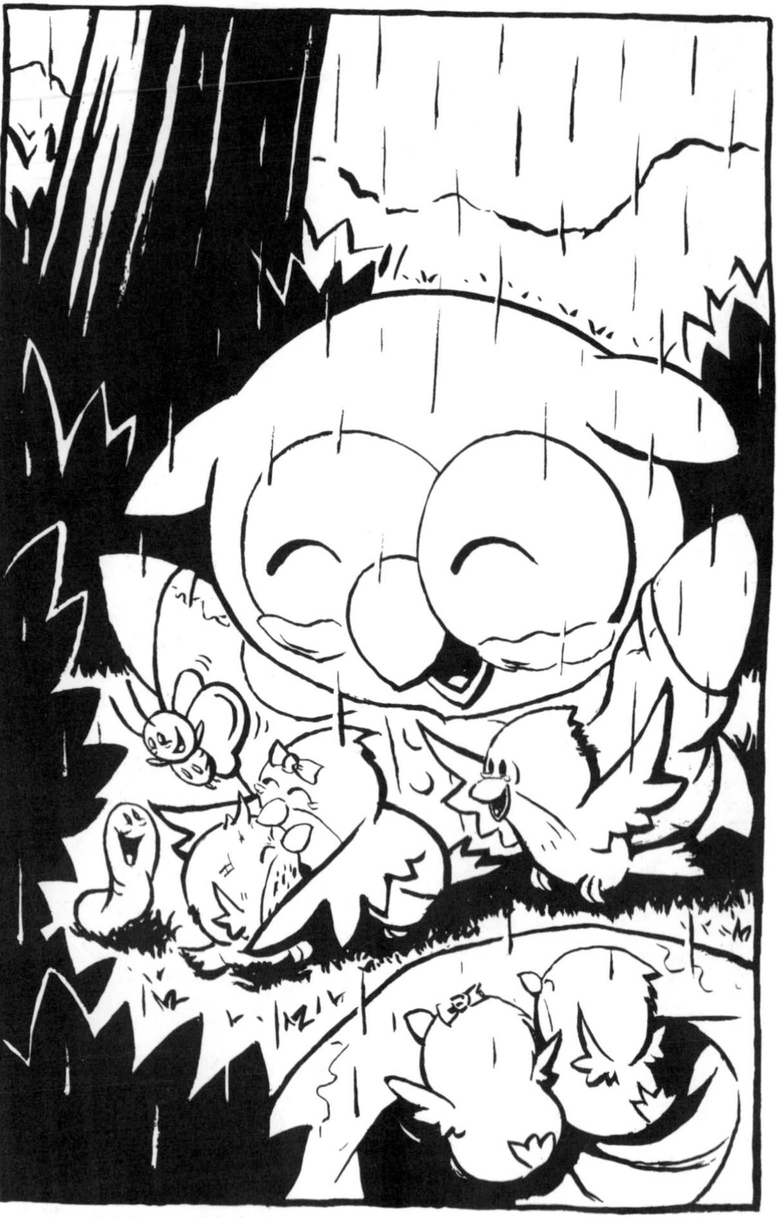

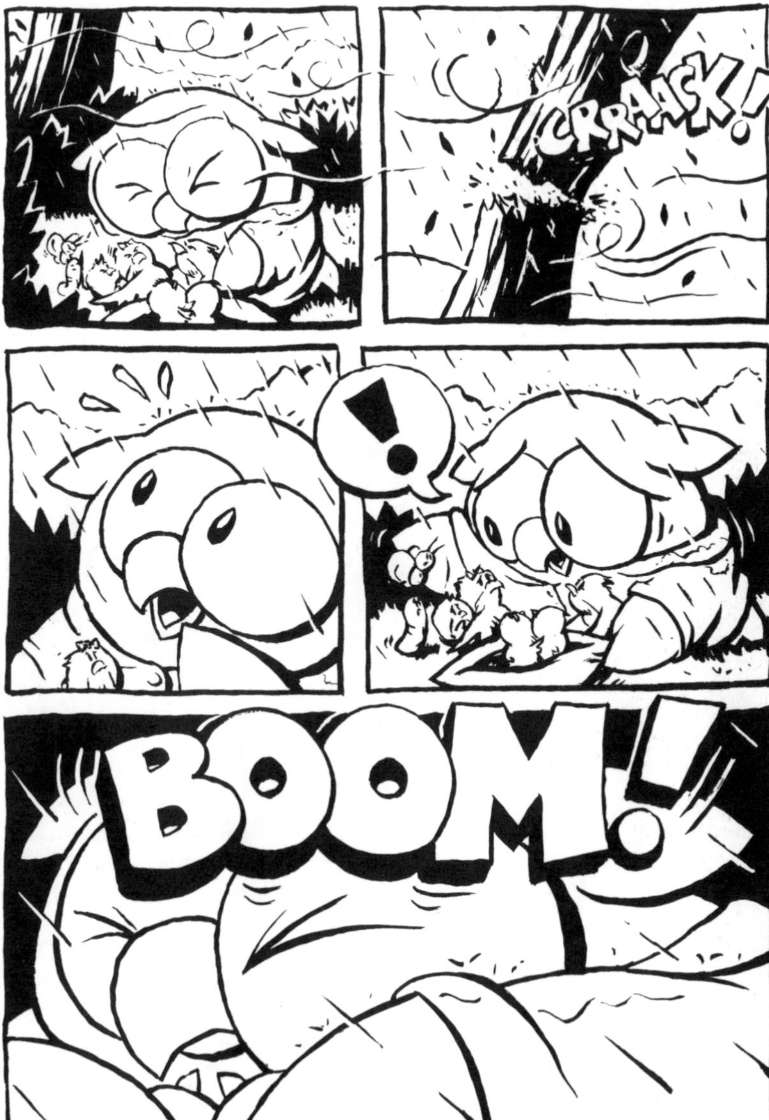
CRRAACK!
!
BOOM!!

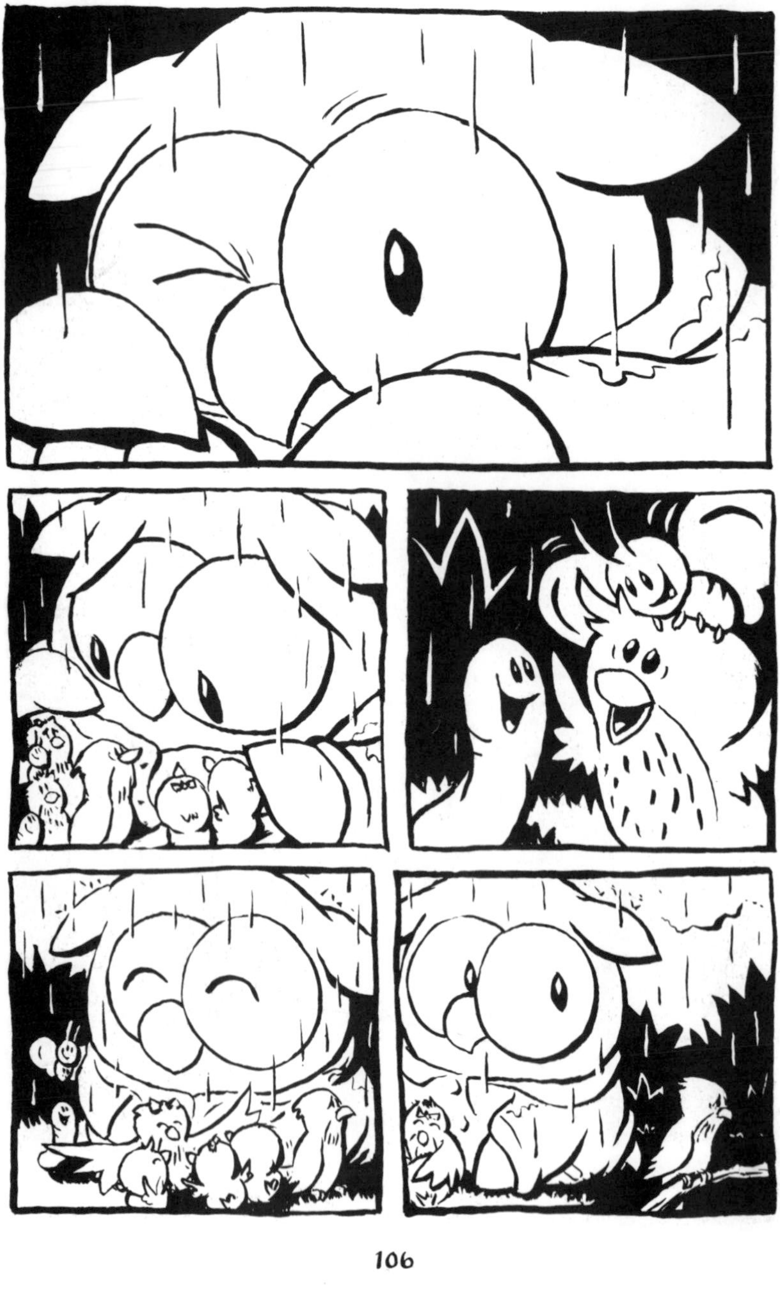

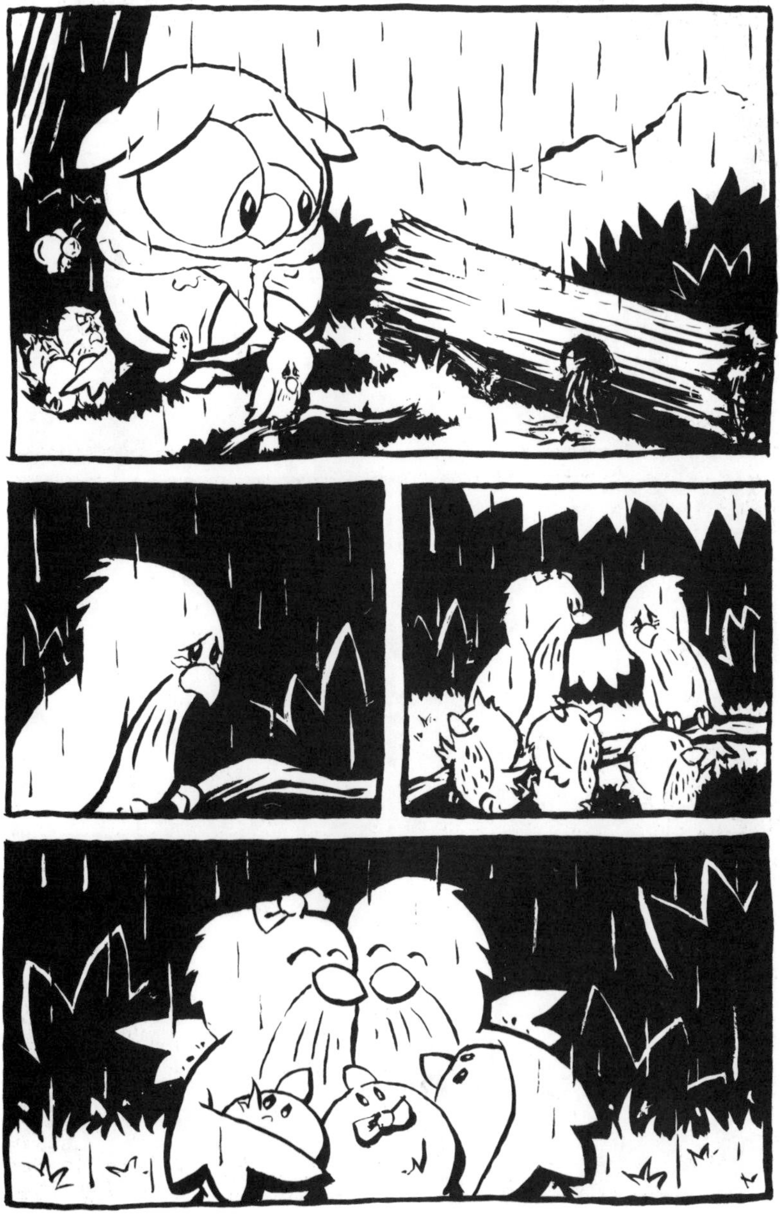

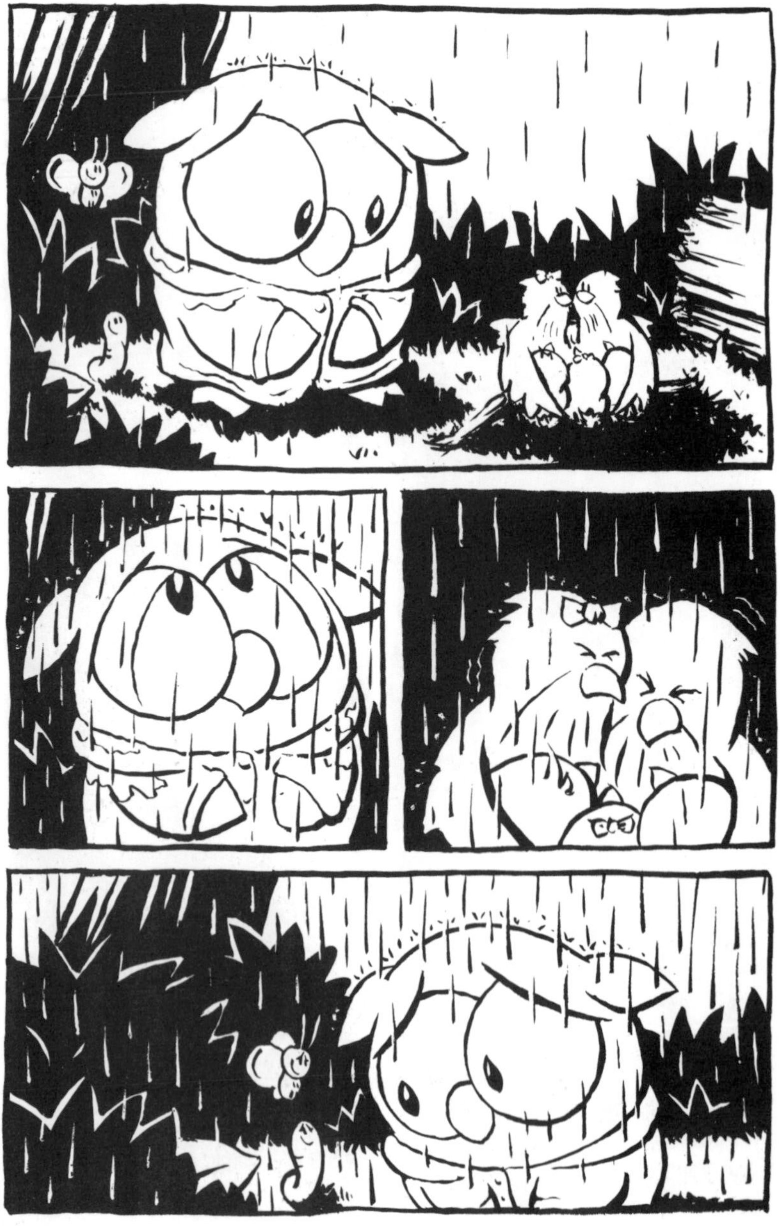

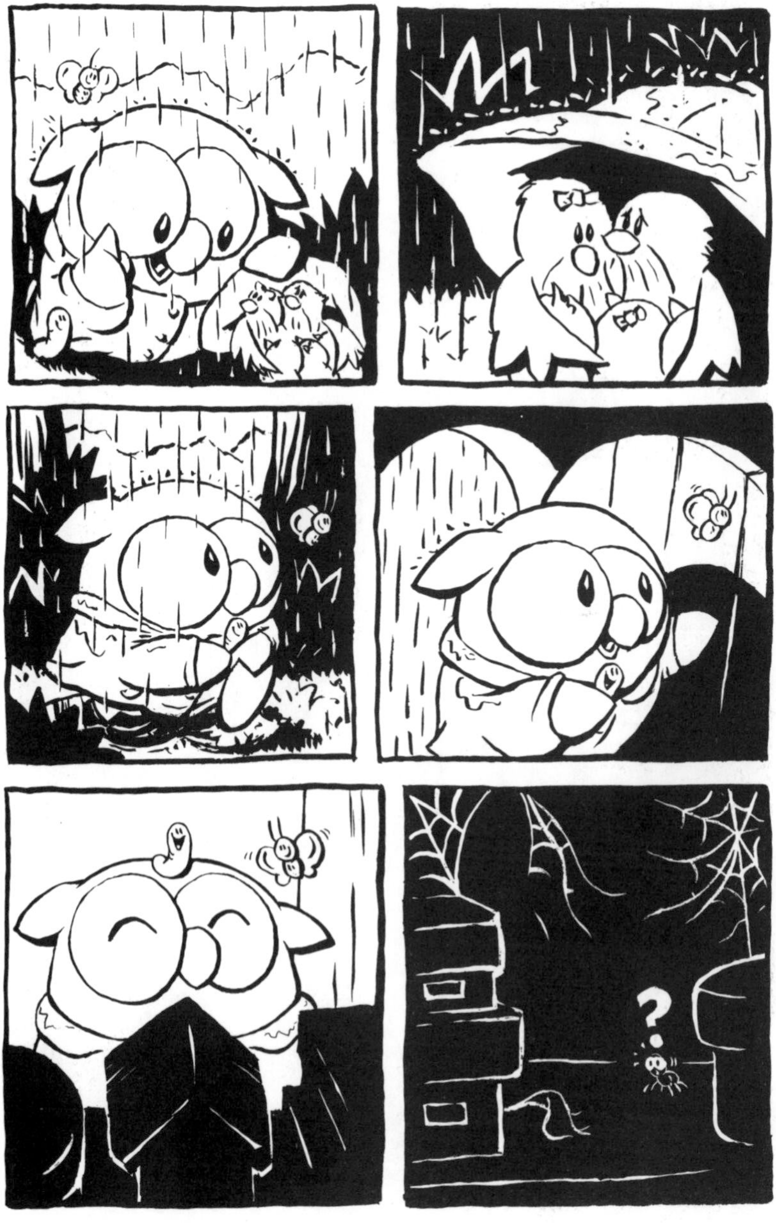
?

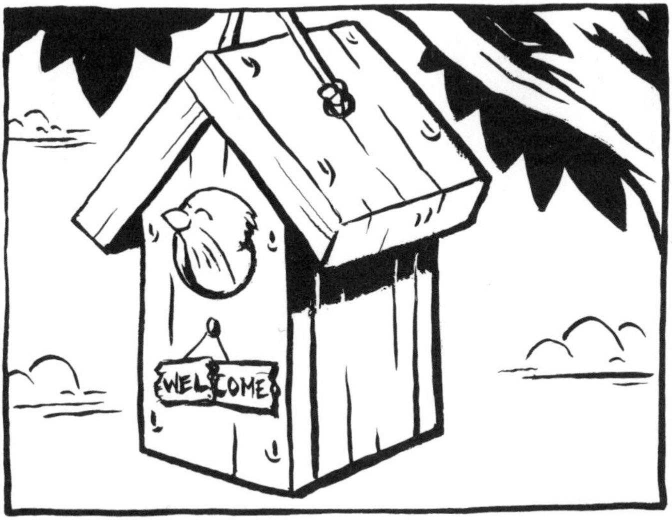
WELCOME

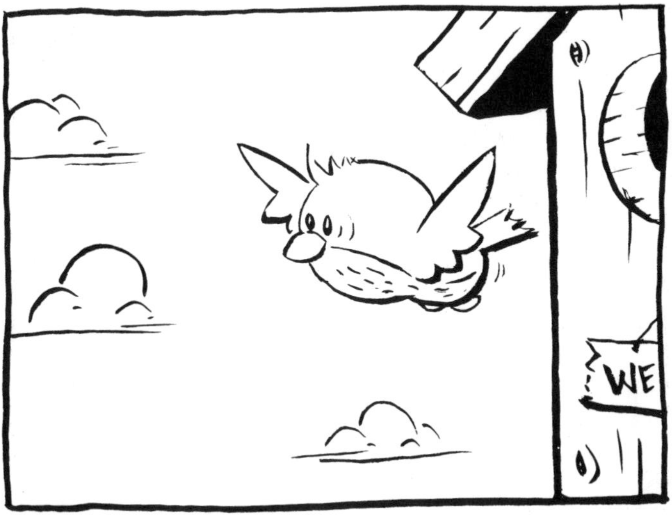
WE

# THE END

Flutter, Wormy, and Little Blue

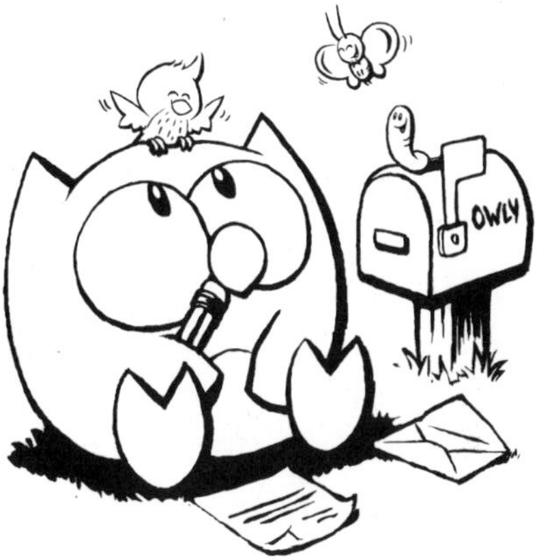
OWLY

: ANDYRUNTON@MAC.COM

: ANDY RUNTON
5502 EAST WIND DR.
LILBURN, GA 30047-6410
U.S.A.

WWW.ANDYRUNTON.COM

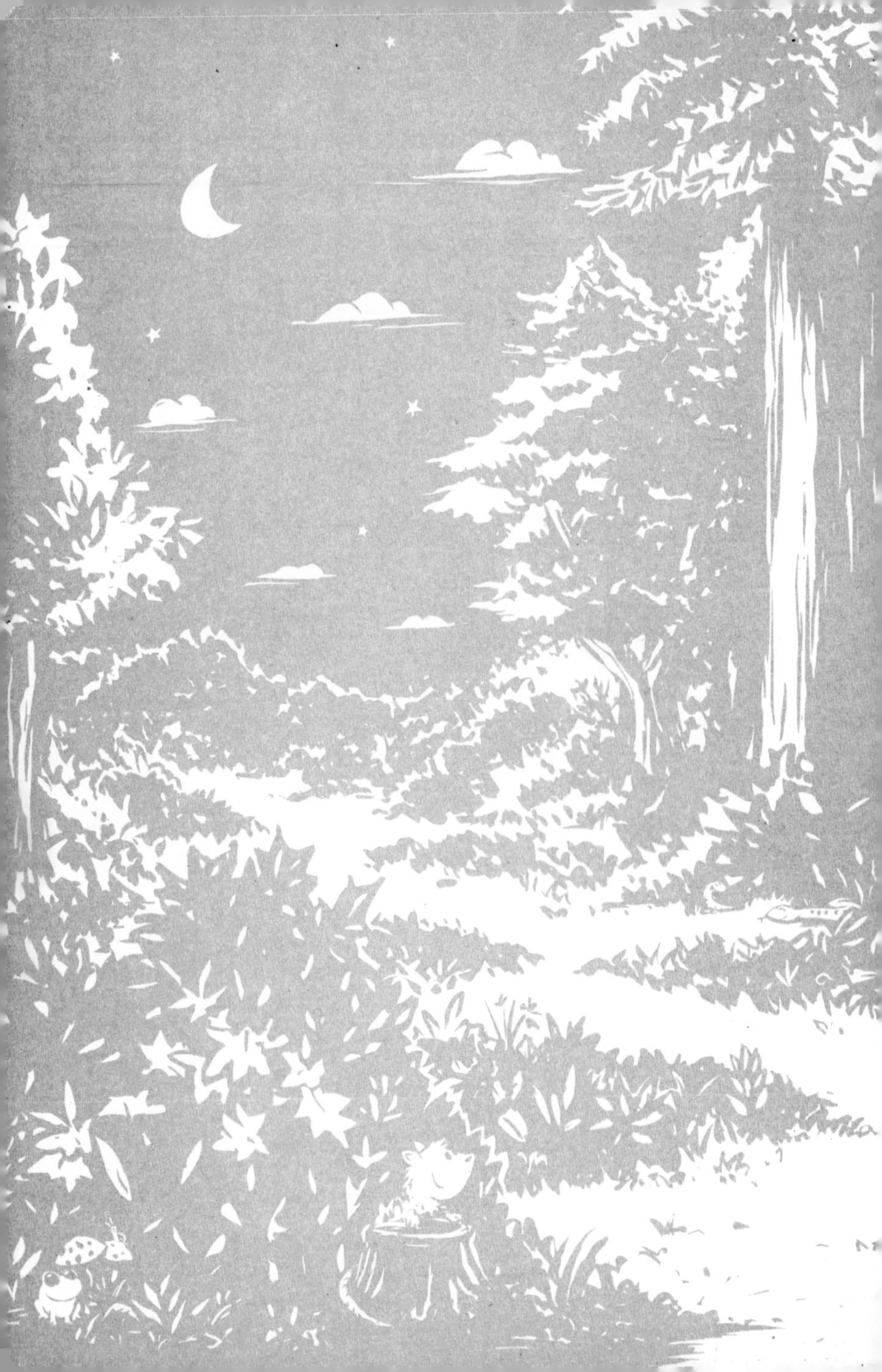